Holiday Sweet Treats

Cinnamon Kissed

Sweetheart

Pumpkin Spiced Love

Jacqueline Carmine

Copyright © 2025 by Jacqueline Carmine

ISBN: 9798289795694

Imprint: Independently published

All rights reserved.

No portion of this book may be reproduced in any form without written permission from the publisher or author, except as permitted by U.S. copyright law.

Contents

Cinnamon Kissed

Sweetheart

Pumpkin Spiced Love

Cinnamon Kissed

Jacqueline Carmine

Gabriella

"Dashing through the streets. In my brand-new shiny shoes! Over the crosswalk we go. Laughing all the way!" I sang as I marched down the street in my Louboutin's. The red bottom heels striking the sidewalk with sharp taps.

December 21st was here, and I was tickled pink that Christmas was only four days away. My first one since moving to Atlanta. I had felt displaced at first, adjusting to the constant influx of sounds. My apartment walls are thin and life in the city is much louder than it was back in Michigan.

Despite always feeling out of place in my small hometown it had taken a few months to adjust to city life. Ambition had taken me far from the corn fields of the Michigan thumb and now with my favorite holiday approaching

I finally felt like I was home. Even if there were three calls for snow since the beginning of December without a single snowflake in sight.

At least I could still wear my heels. Trust me, no one looks good in snow boots. They make my feet look like bricks.

Smiling at the jingling sound of the coffee shop door as I enter, I tilt my head back and breathe in the smell of freshly ground coffee. Hazelnut, nutmeg, and cinnamon assault my nose, and I grin as I take my place in line. There is a reason this is my favorite bean shop in the city. It confuses my coworkers that I always volunteer for coffee runs when we have a posse of interns to do our bidding. They just don't understand that it's a break from the numbers and the ass kissing that every intern tries to employ.

Minutes later I have my peppermint mocha in hand and four lattes for my fellow worker bees to boot. Standing at the curb I check my phone. I scheduled a rideshare before I had ordered the drinks. Everyone wants their coffee hell hot and while I had enjoyed the brief break from the office, I have a manuscript waiting on my desk. It isn't going to edit itself. If only.

The car description is a black Chevy Tahoe and the driver's name is Travis. I scan the street and spot the car parked in front of a dry cleaners. Any further down and I wouldn't have seen it.

"All these parking spaces and that's the one you choose," I mutter.

I didn't expect red carpet treatment but using the coffee shop's parking lot seemed like a no brainer to me.

I might not be a southern bell, but I have mastered the art of passive aggression. As I climb in the backseat of the car, I greet the driver.

"Hey Travis! Sorry about the wait but you were parked quite a distance from the coffee shop. Gave me quite a workout so early in the day." I smile as I buckle myself in and look up to see the man staring.

He is wearing black slacks and a navy-blue button-down shirt, and he has chestnut brown hair that is shaved on the sides and tousled into messy waves stopping just above his ears. The stubble peppering his jaw is a shade lighter. His blue eyes stare at me as though he is attempting to burn a hole in my forehead.

Despite his unfortunate personality he is a gorgeous man. The type that should be on magazine covers and starring in Gillette commercials, not working as an independent contractor driving strangers around the city. I am completely jealous that his skin looks better than mine. I am currently using a new moisturizer that promises to repair sun damaged skin. Meanwhile this suntanned stranger probably doesn't even use sunscreen. Infuriating.

We both are quiet for a moment before I notice his phone mounted on the dashboard is in the middle of an update.

"Oh, my bad," I apologize and rattle off the office's address. Memorized thanks to rideshares and food deliveries. Seeing his blank look, I quickly add, "It's actually right across the street from that new Thai restaurant if that helps. Or I could just give you directions if you prefer."

"No. That's alright," he finally replies.

As he finally pulls away from the curb and begins driving, I take a deep breath. Awkward encounters are my least favorite part of rideshares. I take a deep drink and let the Christmas in a cup bring me back into the moment. Five minutes later we are almost back at the office when my phone rings. Glancing at the screen I see that it's an unknown caller.

Prepared for the usual prerecorded message about my nonexistent car's extended warranty I answer.

"Hello." Polite but bored, circa my call center job during college.

"Hi, is this Gabriella Reid?" a breathy male voice greets me.

"Yes, it is. Who is this?" I reply.

"Sorry to bother you but, I'm Travis, your driver. Just wanted to apologize for the delay, traffic was a nightmare on the way over, but I'm outside the coffee shop now and I'm ready whenever you are," he says.

A pit forms in my stomach. If I'm not in a rideshare, then whose car am I in?

"Uh," I begin. "I'm sorry but I've made other plans. Sorry for wasting your time."

"Oh no, that's okay. I was late. Have a blessed day," he says as he hangs up.

I feel shame color my cheeks. Glancing out the window I note that we are still going the correct way to my office. Luck is on my side. It doesn't look like I have gotten into a killer's car. Hell I am lucky he hasn't thrown me out of his car or yelled at me. He has taken my presence in stride without fussing. I have practically taken him hostage.

It takes another minute of me guzzling my mocha for strength before I can address the random stranger who I have forced to drive me to work.

"Thank you for driving me," I say. "I'm sorry about the mix up."

"You're welcome," he says.

"You know you really should have told me you weren't my driver," I can't resist saying.

Honestly, he could have said *anything*. Anything to prevent this embarrassing disaster.

"Well, it's not every day that a beautiful woman climbs inside my car and berates me for giving her a workout," he replies with a grin.

Feeling my face warm for the second time, I count myself lucky that my embarrassment is mild. I can't blame this man for my mistake. No matter how tempting it is to shift the blame off my shoulders and onto his. I am fortunate he is kind enough to drive me back to work.

"Here we are," the man says as he parks in front of my office building.

"Thanks again," I say reaching into my purse and grabbing my wallet. Thumbing through, I select a few bills that cover what I would have paid Travis. Despite his protests I force the money into his hand. I notice as I grab his hand that he has thick calluses on his palms.

"This really ain't necessary," he argues. "I was going this way anyway."

"I forced myself into your car. This should cover gas," I insist.

Grabbing the door handle I am turning to exit when he spins around and drops the money back into my purse.

"You have to let me pay you back!" I yell.

"Why is this so important to you?" he yells back. "I'm just trying to be nice! Ain't that what Christmas is all about?"

"Well yes. But I was so rude to you!" I say.

For a moment we stare at each other, neither willing to back down. I see tan skin peaking through the unbuttoned collar of his shirt, and it distracts me for longer than I will ever admit.

"You know what? Let me buy you dinner then," I say, waiting for him to scoff at my invitation. I blame the shirt.

For another moment he doesn't speak. His eyes dip to look at my legs and then slowly rise back to my face. He doesn't even bother to hide the fact he is checking me out. My cheeks began to burn as he remains silent.

"Text me when you leave work. You look like the type to burn the midnight oil," he says as he whips out a business card and a pen, quickly scrawling out his personal number on the back.

"I'll meet you here," he says, handing me the business card.

Nodding and refusing to make eye contact I quickly scramble out of his SUV with a quick, "See you later."

Oliver

I waited for the petite redhead to enter the office building before pulling back into traffic. She was something else. My brain had short circuited when she had climbed into the back seat.

Her red hair was pinned up with just a few strands framing her face. Bright blue eyes were framed by large glasses and when she turned her gaze to mine she was all business. Even with a smile on her face she was direct and demanding. She was dressed in business professional with her sweater and pencil skirt, but those heels were tall stilettos. The kind she could wear to dinner and to bed.

It is really no surprise I caved and drove her back to her job. The entire ride I was cursing myself as a fool. The attractive woman bossing me around had flipped a switch I didn't know I had. Any other time I would have explained the mix up and politely asked the unwanted passenger to escort themselves to the sidewalk.

With her I was tongue tied. I didn't even laugh when her actual driver called her. A small smile had stretched across my face before I could stop it. I had to tilt my chin to keep her from seeing it in the rearview mirror. But as I contained my humor, I saw her cheeks flush with embarrassment and guilt stripped away my smirk.

Her arrogance had drained away, and I was left with an uneasy feeling in the pit of my stomach. Glancing in my rear-view mirror I saw her fidgeting with her coffee cup and the strap of her purse. I didn't want her to lose that self-assured attitude.

Like the world was hers for the taking and it just didn't know it yet.

Then she tried to pay me. All her arrogance surging to the front like it had never left. Like I was going to take her money for a five-minute ride. My mother would have skinned me and framed my hide.

Her purse was Prada, a twin to my sister Penelope's. My brother-in-law had complained a little too loudly about the price. Pen had gone back and bought the same purse in a different color out of spite and given a third one to our mom.

Darren never complained about a price tag again. Wise man.

The red bottomed shoes and designer handbag were dead giveaways that my feisty little stowaway was into the finer things. Probably spent more on her clothing than her rent. The type of girl I would never date.

Until now.

I was trying to be smooth when dropping her off at the office building. I was gonna give her my business card and invite her out for a drink. But first we had fought over her paying me. Utterly ridiculous. And then she beat me to the punch.

Her dinner invitation was unexpected to say the least. Never thought I would meet my match outside a coffee shop. I didn't even get her name, or properly introduce myself.

Merging my SUV onto Peachtree Boulevard I remind myself that at least she has my business card. Glancing at my phone on the dash I wonder how long it will take her to reach out.

Gabriella

Oliver Greene is the chief financial officer of Greene Agriculture according to his business card. A quick google search confirmed his identity, and not much else. The man doesn't have any social media accounts. Just a few articles in the Atlanta Journal-Constitution with a few quotes about growing the company from a small family-owned business into the national brand it is now. Apparently, Oliver's father had started cutting grass as a child and worked as a landscaper in his teens before starting the business in his late twenties. From there it was a slow build until eventually Oliver took over and expanded.

All signs point to a wholesome well-rounded family-oriented man. He had complied with my demands and been a gentleman even when I was in the wrong. Absolutely not my type. I don't date finance guys. I don't date nice guys. Since moving to Atlanta, I haven't dated period. But here I was asking a random man on a date. I'm going to blame it all on the holiday spirit. It has gotten into my head and made me act like I'm in a Hallmark movie. Bunch of nonsense.

Doesn't stop me from texting him.

I'll be done around seven.

A few minutes later my phone dings.

I'll be there.

One dinner can't hurt. I owe him after all. And that button down was deliciously tight when he had twisted around to talk to me in the car. No, one dinner couldn't hurt. I thought about texting him again but decided against it. I could properly introduce myself in person.

It's ten after seven when I walk out of the office building. I didn't have time to glance around before he was standing in front of me holding his hand out.

"Oliver Greene. At your service," he says as he takes my hand in his and raises it to his lips to brush a light kiss across my knuckles.

"Gabriella Reid. Pleased to meet you. Officially that is," I reply, cursing myself for my awkward introduction.

"I noticed you don't have an accent," he says as he continues to hold my hand.

"You don't have much of one either," I counter with a smile.

"I thought we would check out that Thai place you mentioned," he says. "Nice public place without having to get into a stranger's car yeah?"

I feel my cheeks heat with embarrassment. His grin says it all. He brings his other arm over our joined hands and tucks my hand into the crook of his elbow. We begin walking down the street towards the crosswalk.

"At least I didn't kidnap you," I say. I'm trying to play it off, but his grin sticks, and I'm beginning to feel like a mouse trapped between a cat's paws.

"Technically I would argue that you did," he replies.

"How did I kidnap you?" I ask as I look him over. The man stands over six feet and looks to be in good shape. Even if it isn't all muscle, he still outweighs me. And I'm betting on the muscle. His fleece jacket fits his arms and chest snuggly, and his slacks grip his thighs like a second skin.

"I considered you to be armed and dangerous when you climbed into my car and demanded I drive you back to work. Those shoes could easily be considered a lethal weapon," he says glancing down at my heels. "They do criminal things to a man's body."

"Oh shush. They're just shoes," I say with a smile. I love fashion and I dress to please myself. But I'm pleased by the compliment all the same.

"Said no woman ever," he replies.

"They are my favorite pair," I confess.

A celebratory purchase when I received my first paycheck. It's not the price tag that makes them my favorite although they are the most expensive pair of shoes I own. They're the symbol of my success. Black leather with that famous red makes a hell of a statement.

"I probably should have asked if you even like Thai food," he says scratching the back of his head with a sheepish look on his face.

"There is only so much coffee and sugar I can have before I require real food, and Thai is right up there with my mother's roast," I say.

"Have you eaten here before?" he asks as he opens the front door that proclaims the restaurant to be named *Just Thai*.

"No, not yet. My coworkers have been raving about the curry though," I say as we queue in line to be seated.

"My guilty pleasure is peanut butter chicken," Oliver says.

"That sounds good too," I say.

"Would you like to split entrees?" he asks.

"You don't mind?" I ask in return.

"Not at all. But if you steal food off my plate, we're at war," he replies.

"Noted," I say as the host waves us forward and directs us to a window table. The wooden table and benches are a pale oak worn smooth from use. And the pendant light hanging above the table casts a warm light around us.

Glancing about I notice several framed black and white photos hanging on the walls and the back wall has a vibrant painting of Bangkok at night. Bright neon lights highlighting the river and the skyline.

The host hands us our menus and dashes back to his stand. Oliver waves the menu and asks, "Do we even need these?"

"Yes, I need to scope out the dessert selection," I say.

"Coconut pudding?" he asks.

"Or fried banana with ice cream," I reply.

"Both?" he asks with a raised eyebrow.

"Both is good," I agree.

Splitting the meal was the perfect idea. From the curry and peanut butter chicken to the dessert everything was delicious. I wasn't surprised in the least after all the rave reviews I had heard in the office. What had surprised me was Oliver's interest in my life. I had invited him to dinner on a whim and had half expected him to ghost me.

It wouldn't have been the first time it had happened. Or the tenth. Dating in the modern era is a constant uphill battle. Online profiles are a nightmare and maintaining interest and conversation via blocks of text has never been my strong suit.

Time seemed to speed past me as I ate dinner with Oliver. As cold and detached as he was in the car, he is as warm and open now.

"Do you want to move back?" he asks after I tell him about my recent move to the city.

"No, absolutely not! I may have been raised in the country, but I was born for the city. My heels can't be worn in corn fields," I say with a laugh.

"What about your family? Surely you miss them," he replies.

Thinking of my parents who are currently aboard a cruise ship headed for Cozumel, I shake my head.

"We've never been close. I have two younger sisters and I was the last to move out," I explain. "I might fly up next Christmas or for my mom's birthday but for now I think we're all enjoying the space."

He wears a frown as he takes another bite of curry. Jumping at the chance to change the topic I say, "Since you gave me your business card, I did an internet search."

Looking unbothered he nods. Of course, he wouldn't be surprised in this day and age. Everyone has a digital footprint. Even if his is tiny and impersonal.

"I saw that you work for the family business. Does it help keep your family close?" I ask before spearing a piece of chicken with my fork.

"Yes and no," he begins. "I started out working as a landscaper part time while I went to college. My father had higher expectations of me than any of his other workers. He's always been my biggest critic and will never give an inch. Naturally, I am just as stubborn. My mother had to knock our heads together a couple of times."

He takes another bite of his curry and then continues, "I reckon when my little sister joined, it took his focus away from me. At least until I started handling the books."

"Surely he was happy to have you take something off his plate?" I ask.

"Not at first. His accounting was a mess. He had receipts and bills scattered around his office in a way that made sense to him and only to him. And that was the least of it."

Chewing on my curry I think about the similarities we have as the eldest children of our families. The pressure to succeed and to lead by example.

"My parents were disappointed that I went after a college degree when I could have entered a trade instead. It's always been about money for them, and my sisters make more money than I do," I share.

"Money ain't everything," Oliver is quick to reply.

"Rich coming from a finance guy," I counter.

"Don't get me wrong, budgeting is my career," he says as we finish our entrées and wait for our dessert. "But you can't attach happiness to money."

"No, you can't. I wouldn't have been successful in either of their trades. They love getting dirty and making things with their hands. Construction and fabricating suit them well."

"I can't imagine you on a jobsite," he says and I don't take it personally. My littlest sister asked me to help her find a wedding dress and if I ever build a house, she will have the winning bid. We complement each other well.

"Only to bring them coffee or lunch," I reply.

"I bet you were the cutest one on site," Oliver says with a wink.

I feel my cheeks grow warm and I look down finding it too hard to meet his gaze. I have always been terrible at overt flirting. Swallowing down my embarrassment I take a deep breath and look back up to find Oliver staring at me with an intensity I wasn't prepared to see.

"Thank you," I say in what I hope is a normal tone. By the smirk on his face, I judge it to have failed spectacularly.

"Whatever happened to the brazen woman who demanded I take her to dinner after she commandeered my car?" he asks with a wide grin on his face.

I resist the urge to fiddle with my napkin or spoon as I strive to ignore how wicked he looks when he smiles.

"She was a mythical creature only summoned when Christmas cheer and peppermint mochas are available."

His grin can't get any wider and I'm struggling to focus on anything other than his bright smile. I'm allowed a brief reprieve when the waiter brings us our dessert.

"She was magnificent," he says. "But I think Gabriella is cuter."

"Stop that!"

"Not a snowball's chance in hell darlin'."

His southern drawl hits harder on the endearment than I consider fair. I've never been a woman to swoon over an accent, but the soft cadence of his voice is affecting my train of thought.

I dig into my pudding with gusto. I've never been fond of strange men using pet names but here I am melting into goo when this one does. I haven't even known him for a full twenty-four hours.

Our dessert is gone in a blink and when I go to grab my purse to pay, he flashes me his phone screen showing he already paid online. I tried to protest but he refuses to let me repay him. Again.

Next thing I know Oliver is escorting me out of the restaurant. I don't have time to offer to call myself an Uber before he's holding the passenger door of his SUV open for me and I'm telling him my address.

I can't put into words exactly why I feel safe with him. It's just a knowing that I sense deep in my bones.

"You got an apartment in a nice neighborhood," Oliver says as we pass yet another street with Peachtree in the name. Atlanta loves its peaches. Shoves them in your face they love them so much.

"Thanks. Moving across the country was scary enough but renting an apartment sight unseen was worse," I reply with a grimace.

You can't trust anything you see online. But I tried to find the best apartment in my price range that had enough reviews to seem legitimate. The maintenance crew were mentioned by name several times which gave me the confidence to put in an application and my due diligence paid off.

Larry has already been to my apartment to replace a light bulb. If I had a ladder that could reach the recessed lighting, I would have done it myself. The old man was sweet and pleased as punch that I offered him a pop.

Coke. I offered the man a coke.

The girls at the office tease me every time I call it pop. It's all good fun but I'd rather not stick out like a sore thumb *all* the time.

The streetlights cast a warm glow on Oliver's face as he drives through the city. Traffic is heavy but it begins to thin out the closer we get to my building.

"Where do you live?" I ask in an attempt to keep the conversation going.

He gestures to the backseat where he had thrown his jacket.

"My wallet is in the pocket. Check my license."

Shrugging off his weird response I grab the jacket and check.

99 Wallace Avenue Apt 29a.

"We're neighbors?" I ask already knowing the answer. He doesn't just live in my neighborhood. We live in the same building only on different floors.

Oliver

F ate. It has to be.

My grandpa told me the story of how he met my nana at least a hundred times over. Little details had changed as the years flew by. Small things fading from his memory, but the big picture had never changed. He had known from the moment he saw her that they were meant to be until the end.

I always thought it was an embellishment but now I finally understand.

She had taken my breath away when she got into my car. Stunned me nearly speechless and now I'm sure she has my heart too.

I barely know anything about her past or her family. But I know the way she looks down when she's embarrassed.

The way that she likes chivalrous gestures even though she's hellbent on proving her independence as a woman.

She is holding her own in a strange city and that takes courage. Gumption as my grandpa would say. I think he would have liked her.

I was raised just outside of the same city where I now live and work. College was local too. I thought of moving away at eighteen like everyone else. Finally an adult, I wanted to get as far away from my old man as I could.

An apartment the town over was the ticket. Until the commute became unbearable.

But Gabi moved over eight hundred miles away from everything she had ever known. And it landed her right next to me. A sign if ever I saw one.

She is ballsy and prim in her tight little skirt that grips her thighs and her heels that make her legs look fantastic. She's a fireball packed into a tiny package, and I'd be a fool not to see her for the gift she is.

After we leave the restaurant, I don't give her the opportunity to call a rideshare. This is a date and I have always been a gentleman. I picked her up and I'll drive her home.

Not to mention do my damned best to steal a kiss.

And secure a second date.

When I ask for her address, I choke back a laugh. She's lived in my building for months and I've never seen her once. I could've had this woman in my life since July. I could've let my niece drag her out trick or treating on

Halloween and brought her to Thanksgiving dinner to meet my mom. Fate may have handed her to me, but it sure had a long laugh first.

Gabriella

"What are the odds?" I murmur as I stare at the address printed right next to his picture.

He looks good even on his license and it's not fair. Mine was taken on a rainy day and despite my best efforts my picture is sporting a frizzy halo. His hair is styled to perfection and his polite but bored smile still outshines the grin on mine. Rude.

"So low it's ridiculous," Oliver replies with a grin. "Also I don't do math off the clock."

Looking at him as he pulls into the parking garage, I can't help but giggle. The little giggle turns into a full laugh and then I'm bent over wheezing. I can feel his eyes on me, and I just know he thinks I'm crazy now.

Finally, when I am able breathe, I turn back to him and find him looking at me with a warm smile.

"I know my joke wasn't that funny," he says.

"No. It's just ridiculous that I moved away from a small town where I probably would've dated the boy next door. And yet here I am in a city with over six million people and the first guy I go on a date with is my neighbor," I tell him.

His smile widens back into that grin. His teeth are straight and white but one of his canines overlaps its neighboring incisor. It makes him look more like a country boy than the CFO of a major company.

"You can take the girl from the small town but not the small town from the girl," he says with a chuckle.

As I grab the handle he reaches over and swats my thigh.

"Wait," he orders as he climbs out of the SUV and walks over to my side to open my door.

A shiver goes down my spine and I squeeze my thighs together.

"I'll walk you to your door," he tells me.

I expected nothing less. He's been the classic gentleman the entire night. If I don't count the slap of my thigh and trust me, I'm not going to hold that against him. Not when I can feel myself getting wet from the brief contact.

"Just to my door?" I tease him as I grab his elbow. The fabric is soft under my hand, and I can feel his body heat through the material.

"For tonight," he replies. "I need time to cyber stalk you after all. Make sure I'm not dating a serial killer."

I give him a playful shove and he stumbles a bit more than necessary playing into the bit.

Suddenly his other hand snaps out and grabs my bicep pulling me into his firm embrace. His lips crash against mine and I grab his shirt to pull him closer. He allows me to tug him closer until he's leaning against my body pinning me to the wall. His lips are soft against mine even with the force behind his kiss.

I release his shirt to thread my fingers into his wavy hair and grip the back of his head. With his hips pining me to the wall and his back hunched over to kiss me I can't help but notice how tall he is. The height difference didn't feel so stark sitting in the car or down for dinner. His hands release my arms and slide from my waist to my ass. A squeeze is my only warning before he lifts me up.

His tongue is warm as it thrusts into my mouth. Every stroke, every brush pulls me deeper into his kiss. My head is fuzzy from the heat of his mouth on mine. All I want to do is drag this man back to my apartment and keep him in bed for the foreseeable future. My legs wrap around his waist pushing my skirt high on my thighs. He pulls away with a groan. My legs squeeze his hips as he carries me down the hallway to the elevator.

"Put me down!" I demand as we approach the stainless-steel doors.

"Why? I can reach your mouth better this way," he refuses with a smirk.

His lips are slightly reddened.

"Because it's indecent and our neighbors might see," I argue.

"We'll just tell them you had a bit too much to drink," he says.

I lean back in his hold to see his face and glare at his chin when I see his smirk.

"Mrs. Williams will be scandalized that I couldn't hold my liquor like a proper lady," I reply.

"Mrs. Williams was young once. She'll understand," he assures me as we wait for the elevator to reach us.

He spanks me gently as he walks us inside. I tuck my chin into his chest as the elevator begins to rise.

"I like the thrill darlin'. If you're uncomfortable, tell me to stop," he whispers into my ear.

Untucking my chin, I met his gaze with a steady one of my own.

"Don't worry about me *honey*. I have no problem speaking my mind."

"That's my girl," he says with another pat and a soft kiss.

As the floors pass by his left hand leaves my butt and slips between us to dive between my legs. His thumb strokes my clit through my panties in a slow steady motion. I was already dripping when he pinned me to the wall. Now with his hand exactly where I need it, I'm drenched. Each stroke brings me closer to the edge and for a moment I forget we're in a public place. I forget that anyone could hail the elevator and discover us. I tip my head back and moan as his thumb makes steady circles.

The ding declares our arrival on my floor. Two below his. His hand slips away and I unsuccessfully fight an annoyed groan.

With sure strides he reaches my door before I can wrestle the keys out of my purse. I hear the click of a latch as I finally grab them out of the depths of the bag. I jam the key into the knob so forcefully I'll probably need to change locks. Thankfully Oliver has us inside before my elderly neighbor Mrs. Williams can catch us.

Once the deadbolt is flipped Oliver lowers me back to my feet.

"Nothing louder than a whisper, darlin'," Oliver speaks quietly into my ear. "Be my good girl and I'll reward you later."

He slides his hand up my waist, pausing to grab my breast and then grabs the back of my neck and pulls me forward. He keeps his hands on my neck and ass as he leans down and kisses me.

When our mouths break apart his hand leaves my ass and slips under my sweater to slide his palms against my hips.

Oliver's eyes are fixed on mine as his hand slides up to cup my breast through my bra. I release his shirt to grab his hair and use my grip to pull his mouth to mine again. He finds the front clasp on my bra and with a flick of his finger my breasts are free of the confining fabric. The soft wool of my sweater brushes my nipples and as they harden. Each shift in his hold only serves to drive me crazy as our kisses grow frenzied. I moan into his mouth as his hand drifts to my breast squeezing it gently. With the sound still lingering between us his hand abandons my breast. Immediately missing the warmth I jump as he swats my ass. The slap loud compared to our quiet breaths.

"Quiet darlin'. Someone will hear you," he drawls quietly into my ear.

I snag his arm to pull him towards my bedroom, but I frown when he doesn't budge. His eyes burn with longing as he shakes his head.

"I promised you the door," he says.

I want to strangle this man. It takes all the decency I have within me not to scream at him. This gentleman who makes me burn hotter than the Georgian sun in August.

Gazing up I let my mouth form a pout as I trail my hand slowly up his shirt covered chest.

"You also promised me a reward," I remind him.

For a moment I can see temptation flare in his eyes, but he quickly grabs me into a fierce hug. It's difficult to be miffed with Oliver's strong frame wrapped around me, but I manage it.

"I didn't tell you when I would reward you," he says.

"Well then," I begin. "When do I get my reward?"

My hands have a mind of their own playing with the belt at his waist. I have half a mind to push my seduction agenda but something in his eyes makes me believe he wouldn't give in easily.

"Tomorrow night. I'm going to take you dancing at my favorite bar. If you're free of course."

"I should be done with work at 7 again," I tell him.

"I'd like to pick you up at your door. It's only proper."

"Was what we did in that elevator proper?"

"Absolutely not," he says with a wide grin. "But I imagine that little tidbit won't make it into the story of how we met."

"Only the proper bits." I bite my lip to stifle my returning smile.

"Exactly. Proper today," he says as he leans in close to brush his lips softly against mine. "Sin tomorrow."

"I'll be ready by 8," I tell him as he slips out my front door.

Oliver

Friday drags by as I crunch numbers and manage my personnel. Christmas is Monday and for the first time I'm looking forward to the holiday as much as my employees. I might not be looking forward to the actual holiday so much as the ability to spend more time with Gabriella over the extended weekend. For the first time in ages I want to skive off work. Unheard of. My assistant would have a heart attack.

I'm out the door at five right behind the rest of them. No overtime for me today. I have a date to prep.

A trip downtown to the florist and I'm sporting a colorful bouquet that the man behind the counter swears is perfect for the occasion. I believe him since I know landscaping, but flower arrangement is beyond my capabilities.

Honeysuckle and blue cornflowers are not a choice I would have picked but he assured me that the arrangement has more meaning than a dozen roses. True devotion to my love compared to the roses simplistic I love you. Bold for a second date but I've always been a straightforward man and hiding my intentions has never been a talent of mine.

During my earlier days working for dad he wouldn't let me use the zero turn. Sitting atop the lawnmower was his job, clearing brush was mine. Poison ivy and briars were a pain in the ass to cut and weed from fence lines. And don't get me started on invasive kudzu. But just as common was honeysuckle growing wild and heavy with its yellow and white flowers. No matter how many fences I had to save from the pesky vine, every time I would collect the nectar.

Drove the old man mad.

Glancing at the bouquet gives me a pang of nostalgia. Take the boy out of the country but not the country from the boy.

A quick shower and change of clothes later and I'm ready by six.

Clicking through channels I settle on a Christmas movie of all things. Quarter to eight and while the Grinch's heart has grown three sizes my own remains unmoved.

Unsurprising.

Bouquet in hand I struggle to walk at a steady pace to her apartment. I even take the stairs in an attempt not to arrive too early. That plan is immediately botched as I take the stairs two at a time.

The elevator would have been slower. But the last thing I need to be thinking about as I show up to her door is how she fell apart in my arms last night. A gentleman does not show up with a boner.

"Stunning," I say as she opens her door dressed in a tight pair of bootcut jeans with a Jack Daniels crop top T-shirt. Gone is the proper high fashion city girl and now there is a country girl ready to shake it for me.

"Thanks, Oliver," she says welcoming me into the apartment.

After I hand her the flowers, she raises the bouquet directly to her nose and breathes them in for a long while.

"They smell as beautiful as they look," she tells me before she darts away to get a vase and I'm given the opportunity to get a closer look at her home. Last night all I saw was Gabriella and darkness.

Neutral tones with bright pops of color. A beige rug but a bright blue couch with faux fur pillows in white and grey. Basic cream walls that match the ones in my apartment, al la renter, but a canvas with splashes of paint in vibrant colors hung in pride of place.

And while clean there is a healthy amount of clutter. Books on the coffee table and side tables, knickknacks scattered across all surfaces and photo frames on shelves and her mantle.

I see one golden frame with Gabriella at the center with her arms around a set of twins. Their hair is a shade of red just bit darker than Gabriella's and they stand a tad taller.

"So your sisters are twins?" I ask as she comes into the living room from the kitchen.

"Yes, but now it's easier to tell them apart. Stephanie died her hair black last week and Fiona has been threatening to shave her head in retaliation," she tells me with fondness in her voice.

"Retaliation?" I ask.

"Their faces are identical, and Fiona says that if she has to look at her face completely washed out by box dye then Stephanie can look at her face without any hair," she explains.

Suddenly I am grateful I only have one younger sister. If Pen is fighting with anyone, it's me. And it's never over hair. It's always about dear old dad. Or about giving her daughter too much sugar.

"I don't think she'll actually go through with it. Fiona is very vain, and Stephanie would have already fixed her hair if she didn't have such a cow about the whole thing. She hates it," Gabriella says with a laugh.

Thrilled she is telling me so much about her family I grab her hand and tug her closer. With her pressed against my body I can feel each of her curves. As I lean over to kiss her, I smell the peppermint that has lingered from her coffee.

Her fingers snake their way into my hair pulling me closer and tugging my head this way and that to get a better angle. Her mouth tastes more like chocolate than peppermint and I have to pull away to stop myself from carrying her over to the couch. I promised to take her dancing and dancing we shall go.

Even if my cock is insisting on bending her over that couch and fucking her until she's boneless in my arms.

"Get your coat," I tell her gruffly when she lingers. "We have a date planned darlin'"

"So bossy," she says with a slow trailing look down my body.

Gabriella heads to a room I can only assume to be her bedroom. I would be a liar if I said I didn't want to follow her and do a different kind of dance tonight.

She returns promptly and her puffy red jacket startles a laugh from me. It looks ridiculous with its fur lined hood, like she's on an Alaskan expedition to research glaciers. She cocks a hip and crosses her arms attempting to look upset but her lips twitching towards a smile give her away.

"I'll have you know I bought this jacket in a colder climate," she begins. "Also it matches my boots."

Glancing down I don't know how I missed the red cowboy boots at first glance.

"Well those certainly make a statement," I say after a long pause. It's the only thing I can think of to say that ain't negative. And I've taken too long to make it seem flattering if her frown is any indication. As much as I loved her heels, I hate those boots.

She waves her hand through the air like she's brushing my awkward commentary away.

"You don't have to like all my footwear. You just need to like me," she says.

"Trust me I do," I quickly reassure her.

"Then stop staring at my boots," she says with a stomp of said boot.

"They have glitter," I say. Again not negative. Just a statement.

"They do."

She stares me down, daring me with her eyes to denounce her boots. In truth I think they're hideous but they're not on my feet. And they'll be better for dancing than the heels for sure.

"So I take it you figured out we're going line dancing?" I ask to try and change the subject.

I'm not taking the bait. Fashion trends come and go. My brother-in-law, Darren, may be a fool, but my father raised me smarter if not better. Gabriella can wear whatever she wants, and I will be proud to stand next to her.

But she's never going to be in charge of my closet. My mother's annual Christmas sweater is bad enough.

"I had a suspicion," she replies with a smile.

She leads me to the door and after waiting for her to lock up I offer her my arm. Without her stilettos she stands just below my shoulder.

"We're going to *Dylan's*. And just to forewarn you, I have never attempted line dancing in my life."

"A southern man who has never line danced?" she asks with a smirk pulling one corner of her mouth up. "*Scandalous.*" She adds in a sly whisper.

"If dancing is a bust, they serve the best jalapeno poppers in the city."

Gabriella

Squealing on the inside I watch as we navigate our way back into the dense heart of Atlanta. Dylan's has a dark wood exterior at odds with the bright blue neon sign proclaiming its name high above the door. No line to get in and no bouncer at the door. Just like the bars back in Bad Axe.

A heat wave hits me as Oliver opens the door and waves me through to the inside. Country music blasting from the speakers and a crowd of people on the dance floor moving mostly in synchronization.

I weave through the tables parked near the walls and find one without any coats or purses. Slinging my puffer coat onto the chair I wait for Oliver to shrug his jacket off and then I reach out and snag the cowboy hat off his head. The simple and sleek black hat works well with my red boots.

He looks shocked that I snatched his hat, but then he smirks. It's not like he has hat hair. If anything, it was criminal that he tried to cover it up. I was going to give his hat back honestly. But with the way he's looking at me all smug, I'm never giving it back. Besides a black cowboy hat would look good with any of my jeans.

He still looks hot as sin in his faded jeans and his plain white T-shirt. His tan colored cowboy boots didn't even match the hat.

I turn my back on Oliver and begin walking towards the dance floor. Suddenly a warm arm wraps around my shoulders caressing my arm.

"It looks better on you anyway," Oliver says with a grin. "And now every guy in the place knows you're spoken for."

My eyes widen as he leans in to whisper in my ear, "Wear the hat, ride the cowboy is how the saying goes darlin'."

My face is hot, and I know I'm blushing from my neck to the roots of my hair. Still I manage to take an exaggerated look from his boots to his face.

"Shame you're not a cowboy then," I quip. "Now dance with me."

I snag his wrist and pull him towards the dance floor. The old wooden floor is scuffed and chipped from wear. He pulls me back for a moment and when he takes his phone out of his back pocket, I wrap my arm around his waist as I wait for him to take the photo. He texts me the shot. I'll probably print and frame it later. Our first photo as a couple.

"I always wanted to learn how to line dance," I tell him as we join the line closest to us.

"Me too," he says with a laugh.

We watch the line in front of us to learn the moves. We are always a beat late and we often spin the wrong way, but I love watching Oliver try to dance. He has all the grace of a tumbling toddler. Halfway through the first song we've stumbled and bumped into each other a dozen times.

Five songs later and we've learned some of the more common steps. We might not match the line, but we have some rhythm at least.

"Thirsty?" Oliver asks me during a song change.

Pulling my T-shirt away from my sweaty skin I nod. We head over to the bar and order two waters. By the time Oliver pays I have half my bottle gone.

"How are you not dying?" I ask, shocked that he's not dripping sweat like I am.

"I may be locked in an office for most of my day during the week, but on weekends I like volunteering to take care of yards owned by elderly people who can't take care of the work themselves."

I try not to be impressed. And fail.

"What's wrong with you?" I ask him while he's taking a drink of his water.

He chokes and coughs as I stare at him. When he can breathe again, he glares at me.

"Most are on a fixed income and can't afford to hire anyone. I would have thought you would have more sympathy for your elders."

"Not that," I say with a wave of my hand. Clearly, he cares about them.

I raise my hand and begin ticking off my fingers as I list his qualities.

"Family-oriented, chivalrous, rich, and volunteers to help the elderly." And for the last one I add, "And I can only assume a fantastic fuck."

I look at him expectantly.

"And you're single? What's wrong with you?" I ask again.

He stops glaring and looks at me with confusion before he grins.

"Well I'm not single anymore, am I?"

I try not to smile at his flirtation.

"That doesn't answer my question," I say struggling to keep a straight face.

"Other women don't see it the way you do darlin'," he tells me and when I give him another look, he sighs and leans back against the bar.

Holding his own hand up he mimics me ticking off his points as he goes, "Family overrides girlfriends, sexist, workaholic, too busy, and must be a playboy."

"Playboy? With all that spare time you don't have?" I ask with a laugh.

"Exactly why you're different Gabriella. No one sees me like you do." He leans forward and kisses my cheek.

I grab the nape of his neck when he pulls back, and I smash my lips to his. Like hell he is going to get away with a cheek kiss after that line. His lips are soft and warm against mine.

As I lean back to look at him, I notice his bright blue eyes are dark with desire. Foregoing my plan to try these famous jalapeno poppers, I run my hand down his chest and straighten his belt buckle.

"I'm ready to ride," I tell him.

A moment passes where he is befuddled but when understanding hits, he looks struck by lightning. He grabs my hand and I grab our jackets and my purse as he tows me to the door and then the car. The night air is cold on my skin but not enough to stop and pull my coat on.

He opens the passenger door like a gentleman and ushers me inside before dashing over to the driver's side.

It's a short drive back to the apartments and since my apartment is on a lower floor that is our destination. His hands are on me from the moment he opens my car door. At my back guiding me swiftly through the lobby and into the elevator. On my waist pulling me until my hips meet his and all I can focus on is the hard length of him pressed against my belly.

We don't kiss and I don't climb him like a vine on a tree. No matter how tempting. Our eyes lock and I can't look away. His eyes don't waver to look at my body nor do they dart away to look at our surroundings. As the floors pass by Oliver's steely eyes hold mine.

The ding breaks the tension and I find myself pulling Oliver to my door. I'll be damned if he tries to act the gentleman tonight. I was promised sin and I'll be damned if I get anything less.

My door slams shut a little too loud to be decent at this hour, but I stop caring when Oliver's mouth finds mine. Warm and willing I'm lifted into his arms as I rip my shirt over my head. His lips find mine again as I struggle with my bra clasp. I love the emerald color but I should've worn something easier to slip off.

He pulls back from me with a breathy moan. I can't mourn the loss before he bodily tosses me away from him. I land on my softest sheets. I'm shocked to find us already in my bedroom. I watch from my unmade bed as Oliver crosses his arms and grabs the hem of his T-shirt and whips it over his head in one move. Every suspicion I've had is confirmed. His tan skin is taunt across defined muscles.

Blue eyes locked on me, and a shiver runs up my spine. Without looking away one of his hands goes to his belt buckle. With one hand he flicks it open and tugs it off. I hear the sharp clink as it hits my hardwood floors.

Oliver's lower abdominal muscles form a distinct V shape right above his jeans. He unbuttons the top of his jeans and then kicks off his boots. All the while I'm laying across my bed still dressed aside from my shirt.

He prowls across the bed on his hands and knees until he's between my thighs. I lean back as he rests his hips against mine. His mouth meets mine and this kiss is slower than the ones that came before. He lingers until my hands grip his broad muscled shoulders. Then he kisses my chin and works his way down my neck, stopping to nibble where my neck meets my shoulder while his fingers confidently unhook my bra.

Chills race down my spine as his mouth moves lower. He licks one nipple before taking it into his mouth and rolling the tip against his rough tongue. The other nipple is pinched between his fingers, and I can't stop myself from arching into the touch.

"Such a good girl," he whispers against my skin when he releases my nipple with a popping sound.

I buck my hips attempting to grind his erection against my pussy, but the layers of stiff denim prevent the exact sort of delicious friction I desperately need.

"Needy little thing," Oliver tsks. "You're gonna need more patience for what I have planned."

"No. You need to move up the deadline," I argue. I've been on edge since last night and I need to release the tension this bastard has been building.

"Good things take time," he says against my belly as he unbuttons my jeans and begins pulling them down my legs. His mouth follows the denim dropping kisses and licks along my legs.

"Let's not rush perfection," Oliver says as he pulls the waistband of my panties taunt and releases it to deliver a stinging snap to my hip.

"Fucking tease," I accuse through gritted teeth.

His teeth flash in a smile before he pulls my panties to the side and gives all his attention to my dripping core.

One long lick between my lips before his tongue begins thrusting in a mimic of what I want him to do with his cock. A cock I haven't even seen yet. In mere minutes his mouth has me arching and pawing at the sheets as fire blasts through my veins and my mind goes blank.

He waits for my orgasm to subside before he withdraws his tongue and begins lapping at the mess between my thighs. I'm shaking like a leaf in a thunderstorm by the time he pulls himself away from his feast.

"Still wanna call me a tease?" he asks as he wipes his bottom lip with his thumb.

I shake my head rather than answer him verbally. His smile returns full force before he hops up from the bed to slip out of his jeans and plain black boxers. I slip my panties off before he gets the jeans off and I toss them somewhere in the direction of my discarded bra.

As he resettles on the bed, he palms my thighs spreading my legs wide to make room for his hips. The feeling of his bare skin against mine is glorious. My hands are clasped in his beside my head as he lines his cock up with my entrance. He slides in with a single smooth thrust. It's a snug fit and I moan as he begins to move. Rocking his hips against mine steadily over and over. I cross my ankles behind his hips drawing him deeper.

My head falls back as his pelvic bone slams against my clit. He's gone from gentleman to feral and his sole focus seems to be fucking me right through the mattress.

I meet every thrust with one of my own. Needy whimpers and moans fall from my lips as he pushes me closer to the edge of coming. I fall apart as his thrusts stutter and warmth floods my core as he finishes inside me.

We collapse in a boneless pile, and I begin to drift off to sleep when his voice causes me to stir.

"Hm?" I mumble.

I'm tired and all I want is to cuddle until I fall asleep. He seems to have other plans because he plants his hands on either side of my head and lifts himself up to his elbows.

"I should've asked before I came inside you," He grits out. Eyes wide and hair mussed, he's never looked better. Jerk.

"Read the room," I complain.

Wrapping my legs back around his waist I squeeze him with my thighs. He looks ready to argue and I'm just ready to skip this conversation and sleep until he's ready for round two. Because I want a second round, and maybe in the morning a third. And for that I need a nap.

"I was into it." I tell him in my most serious tone. The one I normally use in meetings not when I'm lying naked in bed with a man for the first time.

"Yeah but-" He begins, and I cut him off immediately.

"I'm on birth control."

After a pause he nods, and I take that as the end of the conversation. I release my grip on his hips and nudge him so that we're laying side by side.

"Now hold me like you didn't just have a crisis in the middle of our afterglow," I command.

Oliver is silent while I wiggle in his arms until I'm perfectly comfortable. His arms squeeze me gently when I finally find the right spot. I'm falling asleep when he kisses my head softly and whispers, "Perfection."

Oliver

Stretching out across the jersey knit sheet I bump Gabriella with my wrist. Her skin is warm in contrast to the cool air. Rolling over I cuddle up behind her and wrap my arm around her waist. She grumbles a bit when I nudge my other arm under her pillow.

"You're too warm," she complains.

I ignore her. I'm freezing and I've found my own personal heater. I fall asleep to her mumbling about headstrong volcanoes.

When I wake up again the bed is cold and I'm alone.

The scent of bacon reaches my nose just as I hear a cabinet door bang shut.

I'm about to slip my jeans on when I notice a pair of grey sweatpants draped over the bed. Grateful, I drop the jeans in a heartbeat. I was *not* going to enjoy going commando in the rough denim.

Padding down the short hallway I'm brought up short by the sight of Gabriella stretching onto her tip toes to pull a jar of cinnamon down from the cabinet. She's wearing my T-shirt which just barely covers her ass as she reaches for the spice.

I chuckle, stepping forward to snag the jar for her. Expecting a flustered thank you I'm caught off guard when she bursts into hysterical laughter.

"What's so funny?" I ask while holding the cinnamon powder.

"They're so tight, they look like leggings!" she shouts as she gasps for air.

I don't have to glance down to know she's right. The sweatpants she left out for me are a second skin at this point and the cuff is cutting off circulation in my calf. They're too short and far too tight but they are still more comfortable than the jeans I wore last night.

Shrugging off her amusement I take over her French toast while she catches her breath.

By the time we sit down at her café size table she's shaken off her giggles.

"Thanks for making breakfast. I never remember to eat in the mornings," I tell her as I bite into a crispy piece of bacon.

"I can't start my day until I've had coffee and carbs," Gabriella says.

She gets up and pours herself a cup of coffee and asks me if I want one.

"Coffee ain't my thing but, I'll take a coke if you have one," I tell her.

"No pop but I do have orange juice or tea," her reply comes from the open door of the stainless-steel refrigerator blocking my view.

"Sweet tea? Hell yeah," I reply quickly.

She leans around the door to meet my eye as she shakes her head with a mournful sigh.

"Orange juice it is then," I tell her.

The little heathen.

Her wardrobe is fine, I can live with it. But unsweetened tea is where I draw the line. Next opportunity I'm smuggling beverages down from my apartment.

"Oh!" She pops her head back out from the fridge. "I do have Vernors," she says with a hopeful lilt to her voice.

"What is that?"

"It's a pop," she tells me.

I raise an eyebrow as I raise another strip of bacon up to my mouth.

Her barefoot does a little stomp and her hair gets tossed in a fit of annoyance.

"It's a soda pop," she tells me. "A ginger ale to be specific."

Crunching on my bacon I shake my head.

"Orange juice please."

Crazy woman. Ginger ale for breakfast. Must be a northern thing. Not my cup of tea but I'll add it to my grocery list all the same. I'll even brew a pitcher of tea without adding sugar. I'll need to get another pitcher of course. A different color for sure. Like how restaurants keep decaf and regular coffee separate.

"What's your favorite kitchen color?" I ask as she takes a swig from her mug.

Her forehead scrunches and she asks, "What is a kitchen color?"

"Like a theme," I tell her. "My mother is into red right now and my sister is going yellow with a bumblebee theme."

"Lemon yellow," she says after a moment.

I nod to myself. Yellow works because my current pitcher is red. Ignoring her confused look I change the subject. Our next date. It's a surprise and it's tonight. Her skin flushes and I can tell she's pleased we're going to spend more time together. Some women don't like men to be overly invested in a new relationship. And normally I'm a man who cools his heels between dates. But with Gabriella I don't want her to question my interest or my intentions.

I intend to start as I mean to go on.

And that's with Gabriella at my side and in my bed every possible moment.

***

Pulling the SUV out into traffic I drove us back to the coffee shop where we first met. After breakfast we went our separate ways for a bit. I needed a change of clothes and Gabriella needed time to do her laundry. I also made it a point to pop out and grab some essentials from the store. She said she wants to see my apartment and I want to be prepared. It's already clean, but I didn't have anything that Gabriella likes to drink. I spent a good hour in that drink aisle trying to remember the brands and flavors she had on hand.

It was late when we finally met back up for our date and the sun had fully set by the time I pulled into a parking space. But I don't let her go inside. I know she likes her peppermint mochas but only the classic winter drink will do for this date, and I've already placed the mobile order.

Her pout is as adorable as it is fake. I know she likes me taking the lead. She's already proven that in bed and out. I'm sure sooner or later I'll step out of line and that she'll put me right back into my place.

Her face lights up with joy when I hand her a hot chocolate with extra marshmallows.

"Not quite as good as homemade but I wanted them to be hot for our date," I explain.

A short drive down the interstate and we're cruising into a light up wonderland. Gabriella begins to dance in her seat when she sees the signs declaring this the world's largest drive through Christmas light show.

I pay the gate attendant and turn the radio to the appropriate station. As *Jingle Bells* begins to play through the speakers I reach over and grab her thigh. She's vibrating with excitement, and she wraps her arms around mine as I follow the road through the North Pole.

"I thought it wouldn't feel like Christmas without the snow," she confides in me.

Giving her jean covered thigh a squeeze I look over and see her looking back at me.

"Thank you, Oliver."

"You're welcome darlin'. But this is only our first stop tonight. We've got two more scheduled stops on the way back home," I say.

"Two more?" she exclaims.

"Yes. And then I have a Christmas movie marathon planned back at my apartment," I add.

She's quiet for a moment and I begin to worry that I've gone too far for our third date. Her hair is wrapped in a messy bun and for the first time I notice her blush reaching the tips of her ears.

"Just don't try to sneak *Die Hard* into the lineup. It's not a Christmas movie," she tells me in a fierce tone.

"Are you sure?" I ask more to pester her than to actually get the movie onto the roster.

"No Santa, no reindeer, no Christmas magic? It's about a man taking out a terrorist group one by one. Absolutely not a Christmas movie," she rants.

"But it does have the music, and it takes place on Christmas Eve," I argue.

I'm struggling not to smile or worse laugh as she really heats up for the argument.

"No! No Christmas theme and the holiday isn't needed for the plot to work. It could have happened on *literally* any other day and the plot wouldn't change," she argues back.

"But it takes place during an office holiday party," I say in protest.

"Change it to a Thanksgiving potluck and Hans Gruber still falls to his death," she says stomping her foot against the floorboard.

Finally I lose control as we pass a snowman taller than a light pole. I laugh so hard my stomach hurts and I struggle to breathe.

Gabriella glares at my form hunched over the steering wheel.

"You're not funny," she tells me.

"Don't be mad. But you made it too easy," I say with a wheeze.

"I'm not mad," she assures me while still glaring at me. "But if you play that movie, you can kiss my breakfast bacon goodbye."

"Not the bacon!" I shout dramatically.

"All the bacon. Gone. Say hello to wheat toast with no butter or jam."

"You're the real grinch," I accuse.

She's smiling triumphantly as we leave the winter wonderland behind and head for the botanical gardens.

We didn't spend much time at the gardens. And we never made it to the parade. All my plans crashed and burned when Gabriella pulled me behind a heavily decorated Christmas tree and told me she wanted to see my apartment.

It was a long drive back to my apartment. Gabriella couldn't keep her hands to herself, rubbing and squeezing my thighs. Her hands wandered while I kept my focus on the road. She drove me mad the entire way home. As soon as the door closed behind us, I was guiding her to the couch. I want her in my bed but it's too far away and I need to taste her now.

Her giggles stop once I have her pussy bare before me.

Gabriella's hands tangle in my hair and she uses her grip to direct my head wherever she wants. I start with long slow licks trailing up her slit and rubbing against her clit with my broad tongue. Her hands twist my hair tightly and she pulls me closer. I dip my tongue into her pussy and savor her taste as she groans above me. Impatient little brat. I've been envisioning this woman coming apart under my tongue all day long. Dying for a taste. She's not going to rush me. To soothe her I flick my tongue rapidly against her clit for a minute.

Her thighs clamp on my head and her ankles cross behind my head locking me in place. I hum against her lips, and I use my grip on her ass as leverage to pull my mouth slightly away.

"Don't tease me you asshole!" she shouts as she releases her grip on my hair.

Long strokes with my tongue bring her hands back to my hair. I wait for her breathing to become loud and then I switch it up.

My mouth goes to her clit, and I suck on it until her back is arching off the bed. Releasing it with a 'pop' I return to strumming her nub with my tongue.

Her nails dig into my scalp as she presses me firmly against her. My dick is already hard enough from hearing her moans and desperation to come apart in my arms. The feeling of her nails dragging against my scalp make it ache.

Gabriella's thighs tense against my arms and her grip goes from strong to crushing as she whimpers. I flick her clit a few more times, enjoying her shivers each time. Finally she relaxes on the couch I can leave her clit alone and lap at her juices unbothered.

"What are you doing?" she asks.

"I'm not done," I tell her.

She raises up onto her elbows to look at me as I dip my tongue back between her lips. Her pupils are blown, and her hair is a tangled mess. I love how she looks right now. I take my time just enjoying her taste and the little moans that begin to fall from her lips again. I linger between her legs as I bring her to the edge again.

When her hands are back to making me bald, I finally rise to my knees and unbutton my jeans. She lays beneath me in only her soft sweater and as I shuck my jeans onto the floor, I see her hands start to play with the hem. My boxers follow the pants and I swat her hands away from her sweater.

"Don't touch what's mine," I tell her firmly.

The soft fabric slides smoothly across her skin as I drag it up her belly. Her bra is a matching shade of red to her panties. The lacy cups hold her breasts high and tight to her chest with just a little bit of flesh spilling out.

My fingers fumble the front clasp, and she giggles behind her hand. Her giggles abruptly cut off when I undo the clasp and promptly pinch her nipple. Her hands fly to cover her nipples and prevent me from further revenge. Brat.

I lay over her holding most of my body weight up with my forearms. Her hands stroke my chest, pausing briefly to tweak a nipple. Unfortunately for her my nipples are not as sensitive as hers.

Sucking one of her nipples into my mouth has her squirming again. I keep rolling it between my teeth until her muscles start to tense.

She reaches the peak of her orgasm just as I thrust into her slick heat. She writhes beneath me grabbing my shoulders and dragging her nails down my back. The scratches only urge me to ram into her harder. Her breathing is ragged, and I speed up my thrusts as I feel my release getting closer. Muscles tensing I try to hold back my orgasm until her nails dig into my shoulders enough to draw blood. I come with a jerk as she clamps down on my cock and screams her release.

It takes a long time for my heartbeat to calm down but when it does Gabriella is fast asleep. Curling around her warm pliant body it's not long before I join her.

Gabriella

"Will you come to my family's Christmas dinner tomorrow?" Oliver asks as he cuts into his buttermilk waffles. He's leaning casually against the bar in his kitchen wearing a pair of green plaid pajama bottoms and nothing else. It's distracting.

Joy springs up in my chest before reality crushes it into dust. It's too soon. We've had an amazing weekend together but at the end of the day it's still a weekend. Nobody wants their son bringing a woman he hasn't known for a week to a family celebration.

No doubt there will be photos and I'll need to be strategically placed near the edge. They won't say anything of course but we'll all know it's easier to cut someone out of a photo if they're not in the center.

Conversation will be awkward and stilted. I've never been good at meeting the parents. Somehow, I always manage to put my foot in my mouth.

"I would love to," I say as I see his face lighting up with happiness. "But I can't."

The happiness washes away like it was never there while he waits for me to give him a reason.

"I've got plans tomorrow," I say. "But I'm free all day today."

His cerulean eyes stare into my soul for a minute longer before he spears another chunk of waffle and eats it. I'm sure he's going to call my bluff but then he changes the subject like it never happened. In all honesty I'm disappointed that he didn't fight harder for me to go. But then I shake my head and dismiss that thought.

Oliver might not believe me, but he respects my decision. Even if that decision hurts my heart. I'll be alone tomorrow on my favorite holiday, and while that's been the plan for weeks now, I'm feeling a bit gloomy.

"You know I haven't decorated my Christmas tree yet," Oliver says out of the blue.

I glance around his sparse modern apartment trying to spot a single holiday decoration. It's a quick survey and the count is a whopping zero.

"Do you even have a Christmas tree?" I ask.

"Not yet," he replies with a warm smile. "But I'm sure you'll help me find the perfect one."

I tip my cereal bowl up to drink the last of the milk. When it's gone, I hop up from the bar stool I've been perched on and rinse it in the sink. Once that's done, I whirl around with my hands on my hips casting a glare in Oliver's direction.

"What are you waiting for? We have a tree to find! Not to mention decorations, because I'm sure you have nothing on hand." I wave my wand in a circular motion encouraging him to hurry. I do have a surplus of ornaments. I own too many for them all to fit on my tree at once.

Oliver makes a show of taking his time eating the last of his breakfast. A sloth could move faster I swear. While he's dallying I open his fridge looking for something to sip on while he takes the next five years to eat. I never pour much milk into my cereal because I dislike drinking large amounts of milk.

The twin pitchers catch my eye first but then the green cans sitting next to the other pop cans draw my attention. I shut the refrigerator door and cock my hip as I regard the sleep rumpled man hunched over the remainder of his meal.

"You didn't know what Vernors was until I told you." I say. It's not a question but he treats it like one.

"I added a few things to my grocery list," he says with a shrug as he uses his last bite of waffle to mop up the syrup and melted butter that has pooled on his plate.

"You didn't need to do that," I tell him.

I know it's not a grand gesture but it's significant all the same. My heart pounds as the ramifications hit me. He loves me. The logical part of me wants to think my ego is blowing this out of proportion but my heart knows the truth.

"There's unsweetened tea in the yellow pitcher," he says as he joins me at the sink to rinse his plate. "If you grab the red by accident you'll get a toothache."

My vision blurs as my eyes fill with tears. I can feel him looking at me and that's the only reason I stammer out, "Thank you. That's sweet of you."

His hands slide under the long hem of his T-shirt to cup my ass. He tugs me closer till he's hugging me and my head tucks comfortably under his chin. He holds me tight against his chest and I relax in his hold as I get my emotions under control.

"You have a big decision ahead of you," I tell him when I wipe the remnants of my crying away. "Green or white?"

"Green?" he answers. The poor man is utterly confused. Can't blame him, I'm experiencing a bit of emotional whiplash myself.

"You'll see," I say.

Oliver

As I push the cart around the hobby store it finally clicks. Green or white Christmas tree. Gabriella walks lightly beside me. Occasionally she sees something that gets her excited and she skips away to check it out. The space in my cart is largely occupied by the tree she helped me pick out.

A Douglas Fir or so the box proclaims. All I know is that Gabriella loves it and that made the choice easy. She didn't even glance at the white trees on display. She led me right to this one as soon as we hit the store's doors. The branches are tipped in white giving it a snow dusted look. I know she misses her childhood home at times despite all the complaining she does about the freezing cold.

I might not be able to give her a white Christmas, but I can give her a snowy Christmas tree.

One apparently engulfed in decoration if my cart is any indicator. I'll be surprised if it remains upright once she's done with it. The sheer amount of tinsel and ornaments she has piled into the cart could decorate a dozen trees.

And now she's searching for the perfect tree topper. I had the audacity to suggest the first one I saw and that was a mistake. I couldn't care less what sits at the top of the tree but Gabriella has strong opinions on the subject.

Silver and blue star? Absolutely not, it'll clash with the red and gold theme.

Cherub angel in a sparkly golden gown? Never.

At this point it looks like she has exhausted all options. Stars and angels seemingly her only two options.

It's her enthusiastic, "Aha!" that brings my attention to where she is crouched on the ground in front of the bottom shelf with half her arm buried behind rows of the angels.

She pulls out a monstrously oversized red bow with golden trim. A sparkling lace overlay makes it even more gaudy than the angel's dress but I'm not about to tell her that.

"It's perfect," I tell her and she beams a mega watt smile at me.

Her arm loops through mine as I steer our way through the aisles to the checkout. I might not be able to bring Gabriella to my family's celebration, but I can still spend today with her. Decorating has never been something I enjoy but if it makes her smile like that at me again, I will decorate a thousand trees.

***

The tree is visibly leaning towards the right. I've followed instructions as Gabriella ordered me around. Hang this one. Drape this over that branch. Move that one to the back. Yes, we have to decorate the back too! But now my tour of duty is over.

"Darlin', the tree is twisting sideways," I tell her.

She pays me no mind has she opens the next box of tree ornaments. She also seems oblivious to the boxes littered around her perch on the couch.

"Gabriella."

Her eyes never leave the box in her lap. Golden orbs dusted with glitter and red stars also covered in glitter make up the majority of the box. Unsurprisingly glitter coats my hardwood floors. And my woman is hyper focused on her project. Can't see the entire tree for the ornaments in her face.

"Sweetheart," I say attempting to gain her attention once more.

A smile slowly stretches my mouth. Gabriella's been naughty and needs to see the error of her ways. A good girlfriend doesn't ignore her boyfriend when they're on a date. Especially in his apartment.

While she's pawing through the box in search of the perfect piece to add to the tree, I step quickly out of the living room and head to my fridge. Not much for cooking it's usually empty except for drinks most of the time. But Gabriella's cooking inspired me to pick up a few things in case she wanted me to make her dinner. I even got vegetables. The kind that only taste good slathered in butter.

What I want is tucked into one of the shelves on the door. A bright red can of whipped cream. Perfect.

I walk quietly back to the living room and stop once I'm behind the grey couch. Gabriella is still crouched over the ornaments. Like a dragon hoarding her treasure. A tap on the shoulder and she finally turns to face me. Her mouths opens, likely to fuss at me for interrupting and I place the nozzle on her open lip and spray a bit of cream into her mouth.

Her blue eyes open wide with surprise and delight. She closes her mouth to eat the cream, but some escapes and I dive down to lick it off her lip.

"Let's not be wasteful," I tell her.

The ornaments get placed gently on the floor, but she sweeps the empty boxes off the couch without care. Before the last box hits the floor Gabriella has her hands twisted into my shirt. She uses her grip and my surprise to pull me over the back to fall on her. Our lips clash as our bodies tangle. I try to pull away but her grip on my shirt is surprisingly firm. I place a kiss on the tip of her nose and tell her bluntly, "I can't fuck you with my clothes on."

Her grumbled growl is the only response I get but she releases her death grip on my shirt allowing me to pull it off. Next goes her red sweater. It's soft and stretchy, sparking an idea in my head. But I'm not an idiot. If this is designer and I ruin it, she'll have my head no matter how good the sex is.

"How attached are you to this?" I ask Gabriella as I sit between her legs holding up the sweater.

"It's comfy but I have it in two colors," she replies with a questioning look.

Good. A good little sacrifice.

I grab Gabriella's hands and raise them over her head. Her confusion melts away as I stretch the sweater until it has no more give and wind it around her wrists. I tie it in a knot and lean back on my heels to admire my work.

She lies beneath me in her black leggings and her black bra. It has a front clasp and I'm grateful for the ease of access.

The clasp is undone in a second and then I'm feasting on her breasts. Her nipples are hard peaks begging for my attention. For a moment the can of cream is forgotten but once I remember I reluctantly pull away from her delectable body.

Swirls of whipped cream cover her nipples and she squeals at the cold touch. Her squirming causes her to brush against my cock straining in my jeans. I swallow a groan as she grinds against me intentionally with a sly smirk on her face.

"Who is being a tease now?" I ask.

"Looks like it's still you," she replies without hesitation as she swivels her hips and throws her head back. I can't feel much through the stiff denim but with her thin leggings she seems to be finding just what she needs. Pity, I'm not going to let her come yet.

I lower myself to my stomach, bending my knees outward so that I can fit on the couch. My head is level with her breasts, and I waste no time returning to my happy place. Her groan of disappointment changes into a moan of pleasure as I lick my way around her nipple. The cream isn't as cold now and melts in my mouth as I suck the stiff nub into my mouth. I watch as she writhes against me seeking friction. Her knees squeeze my sides as she attempts to run her pussy against my stomach. All in vain.

Her arms are tense where she strains against the bond holding her hands. She can lower her hands, but she can't grab onto anything. Like my hair or my shoulders. It thrills me to see her driven to the brink of desire and desperate to dive off the edge.

I continue licking and sucking on her breasts until all the cream is gone. I could continue torturing her, but I won't. Not today.

Today I want to fuck her on my couch until she screams.

I prop myself up on one hand as I unbutton by jeans and lower my boxers until they sit below my balls. Next go her leggings. I tug them off her hips and down past her knees. But I don't slip them off. I don't remove my pants and I don't untie her hands. This is my show and if she wants to accuse me of being a tease then she's going to get what she's asking for.

I thrust into her with one stroke, and I don't wait for her to adjust. I start thrusting my hips immediately driving into her like a mad man. My hand is gripping the arm of the couch, not the pillowing layer that makes it comfortable to lie on but the metal frame beneath. Her crimson hair is a mess. Tangled and frizzy from sliding against the couch with my movements.

Her moans become louder when I transfer my grip from the couch to her hips. My grip keeps her locked in place as I pound into her. Without warning her muscles lock down tightly on my cock mid thrust and she screams as she comes. It's too hot and too wet and I can't stop myself from coming with a shout.

Reaching up blindly I find the knot I tied in the sweater and work it loose. Gabriella's hands come free, and she wraps her arms around my back pulling me close for a cuddle. I drop her sweater on the floor where it joins my shirt.

We lay on the couch until my dick softens and slips out of her. Her sigh is the only acknowledgement in the quiet of my apartment. Her breath is warm against my collarbone and the only sounds in the room are our breathing. I wasn't sleepy but I'm slowly lulled to a deep comfortable sleep beside the woman I love.

We wake up hours later in a twisted heap. My arm that was wrapped around Gabriella's waist is numb and her legs are twisted in her leggings. I stumble to my feet and help her do the same after she removes the leggings. Her bra hits the floor and then I pick her up and carry her to my bedroom.

Her head rolls gently across my bare shoulder as I make my way to the king-sized bed. Its navy sheets make her hair look brighter even in the darkness. After I get her under the covers, I kick off my jeans and boxers to join her.

She gonna leave in the morning because of her plans. Plans I don't fully believe exist but I'm not going to push her. The last thing I want is to overwhelm her. We've only been together for a weekend, and I can't rush this.

Gabriella

My last-minute dash to the supermarket couldn't be more poorly timed. I told Oliver I had plans and I don't want that to be a complete lie. I may not have any friends in the city yet but that doesn't mean I can't make plans with myself. I had planned out my Christmas weeks ago and Oliver's whirlwind arrival into my life had thrown my schedule into chaos.

Now I need a brown sugar ham and red potatoes. The two things I've always craved for every holiday meal. Simple. On Christmas Eve. What a mess. The crowds are out of control and it's clear that I'm not the only forgetful Freddy in the city.

It's almost not worth going inside. Almost.

But I paid for a rideshare and I'll be damned if I came all this way to turn away empty handed. I'm getting myself a ham with the brown sugar glaze. So help me.

The PA system clicks on, and an employee announces the store will close in one hour. It only adds to the crowd's frenzy.

I merge into the crowd and try not to walk on anyone's heels. The produce section is hopping but I managed to snag some red potatoes without much trouble. Getting to the ham is a daunting obstacle. Children run past me, sneakers squeaking on the linoleum floor. Older men are parked with carts alongside the meat coolers. Clearly waiting on their wives to return with the prize.

In the center of the chaos are two cooling bins stocked with hams. Crowds of people surround both. Some seize the first one they see and leave, others weighing and considering before checking a different one.

"I need at least thirteen pounds Linda."

"It's only for three people."

"I want enough leftovers for a week."

Conversation swirls around me and I squeeze in between an older woman and a teen with a lip piercing.

"Excuse me," I say as I look into the bin.

Two different color wrappings greet me. One purple, the other brown. Taking a guess that brown is for brown sugar I snag the one closest to me. Triumph overtakes me as I read the label. Brown sugar for the win!

It's bigger than I planned to grab but I can freeze the leftovers or give them to Mrs. Williams for her cat. I could stay and look for a smaller ham but I'm eager to flee the crowd.

The checkouts are full, even the self-checkouts and I'm stuck waiting in line for over half an hour. Luckily, I didn't call for a ride yet.

An hour later thanks to traffic and I'm finally back to my apartment building. I dart through the lobby and make a beeline for the elevator. We've never bumped into each other before, but it would be my luck to run into Oliver when I'm dead set on avoiding him until after the new year. It was hard to say goodbye this morning. He was wearing those low-slung plaid pajama bottoms again and his hair was sticking straight out from a dozen angles. All I wanted was to crawl back into bed with him and snuggle.

As the elevator doors open, I step forward without looking and crash into someone. A middle-aged woman with curly brunette hair in an oversized cat sweater and snug pair of jeans catches me as I stumble. Her yellow purse falls to the ground spilling its contents. My grocery bag hits the ground too but at least the woman and I don't.

"I'm so sorry!" I apologize quickly.

I've always been clumsy, but I've never tried to run someone over before. I blame Oliver. If it wasn't for my pathetic attempt to avoid him this never would have happened.

"It's okay honey. Just a little Christmas craze is all," she says brushing the accident off kindly.

I smile even though I'm still dying inside. My face feels hot, and I can't undersell my embarrassment. Dropping to my knees I start helping the woman collect her makeup and wallet that fell out of her purse.

"I really am sorry. This isn't like me," I say, more to soothe my humiliation than to assure her I'm not a crazy person who goes around tackling strangers.

"No harm no foul, really," she tells me. Her smile is warm and comforting. The elevator doors close as we finish picking up her things. "I'm just headed to the store. Like you I have some last-minute shopping to do."

Wincing I tell her, "The supermarket just closed. But one of the bigger chains might still be open."

"Oh no!" she gasps. "The local store always stays open late on Christmas Eve."

Shaking my head, I watch as she whips out her phone to call the same store I left. Can't blame her. She looks like somebody's mother and that means she has a Christmas dinner to cook.

"You're right," she murmurs after she gets the store's answering machine. "My kids are all grown so it's not that big of a deal. They can live without a ham for one year."

Glancing down at the ham I'm holding I make a snap decision as we reach 15th floor. An older man enters the elevator and I step around him to talk to the woman.

"You can have mine," I tell her thrusting the bag out.

Her eyes widen and she pushes it back towards me. "No I couldn't."

"I insist," I tell her. "It's just me this year, and I bought such a large one. I'm sure it will be enough for your family and really, it's too big for just me."

She's quiet for a moment and she stares at me with her blue eyes as if she's reading my soul.

"If you're sure," she says demurely.

"I'm certain," I say with a smile.

This is why I love Christmas after all. The common cheer and doing goodwill towards strangers. If I hadn't ran into her then she wouldn't have a ham to feed her family tomorrow.

She takes the ham and looks at it.

"Thank you," she says. "You know it's not going to be a big affair at my house this year. Why don't you join us for dinner?"

"Oh no I couldn't," I say. I can't intrude on their family dinner.

"Can't share a meal with a stranger? But you can give one the ham you braved the holiday crowds for?" she counters and I sense I'm about to lose this battle. "You said you'll be alone, and I can't let a nice girl like you be alone after you've done this for me."

The elevator dings and the doors open as I search for an excuse. But do I really want to find one. She's so nice and kind. And I don't want to be alone tomorrow.

"Okay," I say and she hands me her phone with her contact list already pulled up. I add my name and number and she sends me a text right after.

"That's the address. We live just outside the city. Six o'clock sharp and if you have an ugly sweater feel free to wear it. We really like to get into the spirit of things," she says as she exits the elevator.

I push the button for my floor and stand there empty-handed wondering how quickly my plans changed. My mother always said I was flighty and impulsive, but I don't think until now that I really saw the truth in her words. I've just agreed to go to a stranger's holiday dinner.

But maybe I've made a friend.

My phone vibrates and I see that I have a text message.

I'm Sandra btw but you can call me Sandy

I grin at my phone and add Sandy's number to my contacts. Not a stranger anymore.

You can call me Gabby

Only my mother calls me that. Despite our differences I've found myself missing her as the holidays arrive.

I'm seated on my couch in the middle of a *Die Hard* movie marathon when another text comes through from Sandy.

How do you like your potatoes?

In truth she can't go wrong with them. If I could live off coffee and potatoes for the rest of my life, I would never touch a salad. Damn nutritional values and meal balancing.

Mashed but with all the baked potato fixings. Sour cream, bacon, chives if you have them.

Her reply is lightning fast.

Delicious. I love it. See you tomorrow!

Her enthusiasm is catching, and I switch to a real holiday favorite.

Elf.

Classic.

Oliver

Christmas morning dawns bright and early. Never one for sleeping in, I roll over and do just that. It's not every day that the love of your life breaks your heart.

Okay so maybe she didn't break up with me. But still she refused to meet my family. That's almost as bad. I can understand her reluctance but the fact that she's not feeling the same headrush that I am is depressing.

I sleep through the morning and just after noon I finally climb out of bed. I debate texting Gabriella, but I don't want to be pushy. I know she lied, but our relationship is still too new for me to demand an explanation. I'm sure she has her reasons for wanting to be alone.

Alone at Christmas. Her favorite time of year.

I wander around the apartment, taking a shower, and shaving. Strawberries and oatmeal for breakfast.

My phone is stubbornly silent throughout the day. My stomach dances when it pings before I leave for my parent's house.

Wear the sweater I gave you.

My mother's text is blunt and to the point. Holidays are her days, and her word is law. My father may have built the company and I may have sculpted it into what it is today but on holidays it's my mother who is the real boss.

Leaving my white button down on I swipe through my closet until I find the sweater in question. Emerald green with large gaudy Christmas lights attached. It makes me itch just looking at it. I drape it over my arm. I'll put it on when I get there.

Glancing at my phone one last time I don't push the button for the ground floor when I get into the elevator. I push Gabriella's floor.

She's not going to like this.

But it can't hurt to ask one more time.

And if she still doesn't want to go to my parents' house then we don't have to go. We can watch more Christmas movies, or maybe bake some cookies. I have been craving cinnamon sugar cookies all month. A quick text should net my mother's recipe.

Or a phone call. Definitely a phone call if I'm bailing on her Christmas dinner. A text would have me sent to the ER. I feel guilty for just considering cancelling on my mom. Dad will just add it to his mental balance sheet.

Probably put it right below dropping out of Peewee football in middle school. The man can hold a grudge.

My mother will understand, she's always been a romantic. I just don't want Gabriella to be alone her first Christmas in the city.

She told me about her work's potluck for Thanksgiving. Soupy mashed potatoes and dry turkey.

Arriving at her door I knock politely. I stand there waiting but the door doesn't open. Knocking again I wait for a response.

"Darlin' it's me," I say to the door.

I knock again and a door opens. Just not the right one.

"She left a little while ago, sunny," Mrs. Williams pokes her head out into the hall to tell me.

"Appreciate it," I tell her kindly. "Merry Christmas."

Her reply is cut short by a raspy voice talking over her.

"Ethel, they're dancing again! I thought you said this wasn't a musical."

Her door closes and the last thing I hear is, "I said it WAS a musical. You old fool."

The heaviness that was holding me back dispels. She didn't lie.

Even more important is the fact that she ain't alone.

Heading to the elevator I type out a text to Gabriella. She might have plans but I still want her to have the option to join me if she changes her mind. I send her my parent's address as I'm carried down to the lobby.

Gabriella

The driver pulls up to a nice neighborhood. Way too nice of a neighborhood for me to be wearing this ugly of a sweater. Bright green with actual tinsel attached forming a Christmas tree.

Her house looks like something out of a fairytale. A wide front porch leads up to a massive brick manor.

"Gabby!" Sandy shouts as soon as I knock.

I'm swallowed in a hug before I can say hello. Her perfume is subtle and warm and her embrace is just tight enough to be considered snug. Reminds me of my mother back in Michigan before I became the black sheep of the family.

"Merry Christmas Sandy," I say. "Thank you for having me."

She's wearing a brown wool sweater with Rudolph the Red-Nosed Reindeer on it.

"No, thank you!" she replies. "Without you, we wouldn't be having such a wonderful dinner."

She ushers me into the foyer and offers to take my jacket.

The inside of her home is just as impressive as the outside. Lofty ceilings and large bay windows make the home feel warm and inviting. Like something I've seen on the house hunting TV shows I binge watch on the weekends. Sandy's house was decorated in neutral tones with modern style furniture. I spotted a white faux fur rug that looked pristine.

When Sandy sees where I'm looking, she says, "Never could have nice things with the kids around. Now they're out of my house and I can finally have the picture-perfect house I saw in magazines. Wouldn't trade the mud stains and memories for what I have now though." She quips.

Leading me through the house she brings me to the living room with a wide flat screen mounted on the wall across a large black leather sectional. Seated on the couch is a middle-aged man with salt and pepper hair neatly trimmed to flow into a tidy beard framing a friendly face.

"Roger, my husband," she introduces.

"Love of her life, I reckon she forgot to mention," Roger chimes in with a cheeky wink.

He stands to shake my hand and while he doesn't loom over me, he is quite tall and broad shouldered.

His sweater is white and blue displaying a beloved snowman. Pinching the hem between his fingers he says, "I can see you got the memo."

"Much better than a black-tie dress code if you ask me," I say causing Roger to laugh.

"Penelope should be around here somewhere, but her brother is running late," Sandy tells me. "You don't mind if we wait for him do you?"

"Of course not!" I assure her.

"Good. He's delightful just a bit out of sorts at the moment," she replies.

"If that's what you want to call it," Roger argues. "He's making a fool of himself."

I raise an eyebrow but don't comment. Despite how warm and welcoming they are I don't want to overstep and insert myself into their family drama.

"Mom, have you seen the baster?" a melodic voice calls from the kitchen.

"Oh, that's Penelope. Come say hello honey," Sandy says leading me into the kitchen.

Where the rest of the house is immaculate, the kitchen looks like a warzone. Dirty pots and pans cover the white granite counter tops and what looks like butter is smeared on several cabinet handles.

A tall and slender woman stands at the oven. Her brown hair is perfectly coiled at her nape, but her cherry red apron is covered in mashed potatoes.

"Penelope, this is Gabriella," Sandy introduces me to her daughter as if nothing is amiss.

Taking a page from Sandy's calm and collected demeanor I manage a polite hello.

"You're the one who saved the day!" Penelope exclaims joyfully.

"That's me," I say feeling a hint of a blush in my cheeks.

"Don't worry about the madness," Penelope reassures me. "It's all part of my method."

Glancing around my doubt must show on my face.

"Just you wait Gabriella, this will be the best dinner of your life," Penelope claims. "My husband and daughter are at his father's house right now, but they should be in time for dinner."

Leading me back out of the kitchen Sandy stashes me on the couch with Roger.

"I'm just going to go help Penelope in the kitchen for a bit. Feel free to have a cookie dear," she says pointing to the plate on the coffee table where pink snowmen and blue reindeer clearly decorated by a child cover a dish.

"And Roger don't make her watch football!" she shouts as she returns to the kitchen.

"*Die Hard* is on," Roger suggests after an awkward moment.

Feeling shy in a stranger's home I agree to watch the action movie. The man is a grandfather who has probably sat through every Christmas movie a dozen times at least. I can bite my tongue just this once.

As John McClane kills yet another terrorist, I hear a familiar deep voice behind me say, "Now this is the betrayal to end all betrayals."

Spinning on the cushion I look up to see Oliver's grinning face.

"I don't even care how you wound up in my parent's house," he continues with a shake of his head. "But how dare you watch this without me?"

"Uh," Is the only sound I'm capable of making as Oliver rounds the side of the sectional to plop down beside me.

His sweater lights up briefly emphasizing the Christmas tree spanning his torso. As he wraps his arm around my shoulders and tugs me closer Roger pips up, "Don't make the girl uncomfortable, just because you got dumped."

Confusion causes Oliver's eyebrows to scrunch together.

"I didn't get dumped," he says looking from me to his father.

"Your girlfriend didn't want to spend Christmas with your family," Roger says with a scoff. "I doubt that relationship is going to pan out son."

Oliver's gaze slides back to mine and I watch as he processes the information available to him.

"I bumped into your mom on the elevator. Gave her a ham. Didn't know she was your mom. She insisted I come over for dinner," I spit out finally.

Silence reigns as Roger and Oliver both look at me like I'm growing a second nose. I want to sink through the couch and then the floor when Roger begins to laugh.

"Sandy!" he shouts. "Baby you'll never believe this!"

He jumps from the couch and damn near sprints into the kitchen eager to tell his wife about the new drama.

"Well," Oliver begins. "It's a sealed deal now darlin'."

He relaxes back into the couch and bumps his forehead against mine. I turn to face him fully without pulling back.

"I just thought it was too soon," I murmur.

I don't want him thinking like his dad. I don't want him to think I don't want him.

"It definitely was. And I didn't think you were trying to dump me. Me and my dad don't usually agree on much," he says as he grabs my nape.

His thumb guides my chin up and he kisses me softly.

"Also you got scammed," he whispers against my lips.

Jerking back I stare at him until he explains.

"I sent my mom the picture I took of us at the bar. Dad didn't know you were my girlfriend, but she sure did," he tells me as his mother walks back out of the kitchen.

"You didn't need a ham!" I shout at Sandy.

"Nope," she says proudly with her hands on her hips. "I've had one in the freezer since October. This is far from my first rodeo."

She looks so smug looking at me and I can't find it in my heart to be mad. I wanted to meet Oliver's family and spend Christmas with him. I just didn't want to seem clingy and overly infatuated. Clearly around this family I'm destined to be the normal one. Roger is second with his faulty movie choice.

"This is kind of tradition with our mother," Penelope says from the doorway. "She invited Darren to a cousin's wedding as my plus one without telling me."

Oliver is looking at me with a direct and piercing gaze when he asks, "I'll take you home if you want. You don't have to stay for dinner if you're uncomfortable."

His calm manner reassures me.

I see the truth in his resolve on his face. He will sabotage his own mother's plan to make me happy, even at the cost of his own happiness.

Deciding to be selfish I reply, "Oh no, I'm staying. She owes me a meal for manipulating my emotions at the very least."

Glancing over at Penelope still standing by the door I add, "And it had better be the best ham I've ever tasted and *not burned*."

She looks puzzled for a moment before she dashes back into the kitchen shouting, "Oh shit, oh shit!" At the top of her lungs.

Oliver and I share a look before we both laugh.

"Well now that I know who you are I have a few questions about your intentions young lady," Roger says as he returns to his spot on the couch.

"Dad," Oliver drags the word out with a groan.

I try my best to smother a giggle.

"Well I can't have you marrying some Yankee who is going to drag you up to the great white north now can I?" He glares at his son.

"I'm settled here," I reassure Roger. "I video called my sisters this morning, but my family isn't as tight knit as yours."

"You work?" Roger asks point blank.

"Copy editor in the city. Moved here for the job actually," I reply quickly.

"Children?" Roger asks.

"Dad!" Oliver cuts in quickly. "We've been dating for five days!"

Roger doesn't argue but his eyebrow does raise as he looks in my direction.

"Far too personal, Roger," I admonish.

When Oliver turns back to face his dad, I make eye contact and raise three fingers.

His smile is brief but smug.

Oliver whips back to look at me but I adopt an innocent expression. It's far too soon to be discussing children with my boyfriend.

"Now can we watch an actual Christmas movie while we wait?" I ask.

"Of course," Roger agrees. "And we can discuss obligations and the importance of stressing those to your children."

"Dad!" Oliver shouts. "It was one season, and I was bad at football."

"You made a commitment and you let your team down," Roger continues without acknowledging his son's distress.

"It was middle school!" he shouts in reply.

Epilogue

Oliver

One Year Later

"Oliver! She's here!" I hear my sister call from the living room.

Penelope's watched for her arrival for the last hour. Gabriella was supposed to arrive at one o'clock sharp. But my wonderful girlfriend has the pesky trait of being overly punctual. We all knew she'd be here early.

And for once I'm actually ready on time. Gabriella time not real time. I swear we haven't gone to a single event without being at least thirty minutes early. And if she had her way it would've been an hour.

So I told her one o'clock, and we planned for noon.

Penelope had a girl's day with her earlier in the week. Katie was in charge of keeping Buster her new puppy out of the shot. My mom invited Gabriella over early to help Penelope cook Christmas dinner. Darren is recording on his phone ever since Gabriella's car pulled into the driveway. And my dad is keeping me calm. Or trying to at least.

I'm not calm. And that's okay. I shouldn't be calm. This day is too important to treat it with any manner of nonchalance.

I hear her heels click on the hardwood as she enters the house.

Tap. Tap. Tap.

"Sandy!" she calls as she walks through the house. "Penelope!"

She enters the living room carrying her casserole dish filled with ham rolls and she freezes. Her sweater this year shares a theme with mine. On mine is Rudolph and on hers is Clarice.

The tree we decorated as a family stands tall behind me with ornaments Pen and I made as children. Katie's latest popsicle art is in pride of place and Gabriella's mom sent one of hand painted ornaments as well.

Standing in a loose ring around the living room is my entire family. Soon to be our family.

My dad steps forward to take the dish from her shaking hands and I walk forward to hold her hands in my own.

"Merry Christmas Gabriella," I say looking into her bright blue eyes.

Her red hair tumbles down her back in loose curls and I release one hand to twirl a strand between my fingers. Since our first days together I have loved playing with the silky strands.

"Merry Christmas Oliver," she says as I release her hair and sink down to kneel on one knee.

Grabbing the ring box from my pocket I hold her gaze with my own. Silence reigns as I open the box and she begins to cry. My hands begin to tremble and I clench the box as tightly as I can to steel my nerves.

"I never was one to put much thought into the magic of Christmas. Bit of a grinch really," I begin. "But then last year the most beautiful woman I have ever met carjacked me and I've been obsessed with her ever since."

Gabriella's eyes are red and she's trying to wipe her tears away with her sweater's sleeve, but she can't keep up with the deluge.

"I love you with every cell in my body and I've known since the beginning we were meant to be. A bit of Christmas magic brought us together and it is only fitting that I ask you to be my wife on our favorite holiday."

She's nodding before I can finish but I still ask anyway, "Gabriella Marie Reid will you marry me?"

"Yes!" she screams.

She launches herself into my arms as I stand nearly knocking me down. Clutching her tightly to my chest I bury my face into her curls as I feel my own eyes well with tears.

I was a little afraid she would say no.

"Congratulations my dear," my mother says when I finally release my fiancée.

I slip the ring onto her finger taking care not to scratch her bright red nail polish. As the rest of the family steps forward to congratulate and hug us my eyes remain fixed on Gabriella.

She's been mine since that first day. My own Christmas miracle.

The End

Check out Sweetheart to meet the next couple in the Holiday Sweet Treats Series. Jill and Alan have been coworkers for years and they've had a prank war going just as long. But Alan has a secret. He's loved Jill the entire time and when she snaps after a meeting he finally decides to make his move. This Valentine's Day romance has enemies to lovers, spice, and a sweet HEA.

Sweetheart

Jacqueline Carmine

Jill

"Did you forget to CC me on the monthly inventory report again, Sweetheart?" Alan asks from where he sits behind his meticulously organized desk. His amber eyes are cold and sharp as he confronts me.

The fact that my own eyes are a muddy brown in the best lighting while his are such a luminous shade only adds to my irritation.

Coming from someone else the name would be an endearment. From him it drips with condescension. Ever since he was hired, he has called me sweetheart and every effort I made to discourage it only served to encourage him. Even on memos and emails he addresses me with the nickname. The other employees think it's sweet. And our CEO, Pauline, is convinced we are dating in secret and that I need to contact HR to disclose our nonexistent relationship.

Thanks to Valentine's Day being this next Monday everything in the office is covered in pink and red decorations. And love is on everyone's mind. So naturally Pauline has sent me yet another memo to set up that meeting with HR. My grey-haired boss is a stickler for rules. She's as prim and proper as a teacher with enough smarts to take a no-name brand and build it into an empire.

It doesn't matter how many times I deny it, she's convinced we're an item. And because it clearly gets under my skin, Alan only leans into the rumor.

A pessimistic part of me believes he gets away with half of what he says and does simply because he's attractive. Tall with broad shoulders and a sharp jawline he makes every other man in the office look short and stumpy. Even O'Neill, the quality manager, who the assistants had previously dubbed McDreamy.

The fact that he's always wearing crisp custom-tailored suits with impeccably pressed dress shirts only adds to his allure and my irritation. I once wore a wrinkled blouse after a particularly rowdy girl's night and the man had the gall to offer me his portable steamer.

From anyone else it would be a friendly offer but the condescending smirk on his face taints the offer with his smug superiority.

His dark wavy hair is cut close to his ears and always meticulously styled to the point of insanity. My insanity. Everyone has bad hair days. Stroking my hand through my own brown frizz, courtesy of another humid day here in Atlanta, is yet another reminder of why I hate him. After three years I have never seen Alan Landrum less than perfectly put together. The only imperfection is a crooked smile that only adds to his attractiveness.

Just the sight of him is enough to piss me off lately.

"No Alan. It was a choice I made," I tell him with an overly saccharine smile.

"Well, I hope you don't need access to any of the Brunstein files," he replies with a pretentious smirk.

When Pauline insisted on hiring another staff member to share the workload I had handled since Everglow's creation I was hesitant to give up my responsibilities.

Pauline and I started this company from nothing. As Vice President I had a lot of responsibility and helping build a skin care company from the ground up had given me a sense of pride and if I'm honest a measure of control. I worried details would slip through the cracks and our reputation would suffer.

I was also a tiny bit bitter that he was stepping into Everglow as my equal. But in a few months that feeling faded. Alan Landrum might be a condescending jackass, but he is nothing if not thorough. I can handle petty office games and playground insults. The tradeoff is well worth it, and he has earned his place here.

I'll die before I tell him that though.

The day passes like every other before it. Alan offers me a cup of coffee when he fetches his own, the twist being that it's tepid at best. He always makes sure to do this in front of Pauline so that he appears chivalrous. It also adds fuel to the dating rumor. We attend meetings on quarterly reports and product pitches. Alan makes sure to sit closer to the presenter at each meeting and every time I shift my seat to get a better view, he is quick to mimic my movement to block my line of sight again.

This is all low-level hazing of course. Not even close to some of his more devious pranks. Like calling my mother and asking her to send me a singing telegram for my birthday because I was feeling down lately. He made sure she sent it to the office and even recommended a time when we were in a shareholder meeting. I almost killed him.

Then there was the time when he swapped my work laptop for one that was factory reset on the same day that my reports were due. I spent half the day with IT trying to figure out my passwords. All different and unique and completely unrememberable and all saved on my other computer. A computer I thought had lost all my data. Once I realized that my laptop didn't have a mangled USB port on the side, I realized Alan's duplicity. But the bastard refused to tell me where he stashed my laptop. I spent the second half of my day looking for my laptop and when I finally found it, I had to rush to get all my reports done. I didn't leave the office until 2 AM that night.

So now I consider condescension and his piss poor barista skills as normal office behavior. Hell, it's almost polite at this point.

Double checking my email, I see that Pauline does indeed want me to work on the Brunstein files today. Smug bastard. The folder sits on his desk in open view and every so often he moves it a little to the right or to the left just to see if I'm paying attention. I do my best to ignore his little game.

Finally at noon, Pauline exits her office, and I launch my plan.

"Alan?" I called a little loudly over to my coworker.

His head comes up from the paper he was reading, and I can see his eyes are narrowed. But I've gotten Pauline's attention, and he knows it.

"I just got a notification from the app that my food order is here. Could you be a lamb and go pick it up from the lobby for me?" I ask sweetly.

He glances at our boss before acquiescing and joins her as she leaves on her lunch break. I knew he couldn't refuse in front of her. Alan is all about upward mobility and rank climbing. Can't get a promotion if you are snarky and rude. At least you can't get a promotion if your boss *knows* that you're snarky and rude.

I have the file in hand a second after the elevator door closes and quickly rush to the printer to make copies. The folder is back on his desk exactly where he left it and I have my own copy before he can make his return.

When he returns empty handed as I knew he would he gives me an odd look before commenting, "Your food wasn't there."

"Oh, I forgot to order. Silly me," I say without looking up from my work.

"How did you get a notification for an order you didn't make?" he asks skeptically.

"Old notification. You know how ditzy I can be," I say flicking my hand down like I'm swatting a fly.

"Of course, Sweetheart," his deep voice rumbles and while I'm tempted to peek and see if he's smirking again, I resist.

All goes according to plan until it doesn't.

Alan

If I could have created my ideal woman, it would not be Jill Sweeny. She's gorgeous, no doubt, but I can't claim love at first sight. Lust on the other hand is another matter. Her curvy body distracted me daily, add in her mahogany brown hair that is always just a little messy and her pouty pink lips and she was the star of all my fantasies come to life.

My body desired her, but she was unrelentingly brutal, and my mind wasn't on board. Nothing like the soft and sweet woman of my dreams. My first year at Everglow was nigh on unbearable. Jill is a hard taskmaster, and her expectations are ridiculously high.

She's a perfectionist when it comes to her work, but her surroundings and personal appearance are another matter entirely. She has multiple plants at her desk and several knick-knacks adding to the cluttered space. No discernable organization system. No color coding or anything else. The disparity is enough to set me on edge.

To cope I slowly started working my way under her skin. I brewed the most bitter coffee possible and served it to her lukewarm and then I told everyone in the office that Jill preferred it that way. I switched out her laptop one day for one that was factory reset. The panic that I watched her go throughout the day as she tried to remember her passwords had me grinning from ear to ear.

I was sure my antics would get me fired. Several times I expected it. But she never reported me. Instead, she retaliated. Each action I took against her, she met with equal fervor.

That hasn't changed in the three years since my first day.

But my opinion did. Not all at once but slowly she won my respect. And then my heart. The gentle woman in my fantasies morphed from a simple sweet figure into a small woman with an aggressive attitude and a sharp tongue.

I remember the long hours she put in, staying after everyone left. The accounts she managed single-handedly, the sheer amount of paperwork that crossed her desk every day. And once I realized my position only existed to split the job she had managed to do alone for *years* she had my respect.

And that she did it without a solid support system blew my mind. I found out from Pauline that Jill's parents died when she was in her early twenties. Jill doesn't talk about it, but Pauline asked me to make sure that Jill didn't overwork herself. It became an unofficial part of my job to make sure she left the office at a reasonable hour every day. She's 100% drive without any brakes.

Her expectations were high because she held herself to a higher standard. Everything I did she had done better. She was unrelenting because I was doing half the job she normally did, and I wasn't meeting her standards.

Never one to back down from a challenge, I rose to meet her standards and slowly I started my pursuit. The pranks lost their malicious edge, and I started thinking of her as my sweetheart. I'll never tell her but the first time I slipped up and called her Sweetheart to her face she turned the lightest shade of pink, and I was fully enamored.

Now, the only person who doesn't realize I'm completely in love with her is herself. Not for lack of trying on my part.

I could tell her straight. But I don't want a flat-out rejection. Company policy says I have one chance to ask her out. Then if I ask again, it will be considered harassment, so my one shot has to count. I've watched for signs that she feels the same way I do for years.

And every Valentine's Day I do something more direct. A small signal of my affection, a feeler that I extend to see if she shares the same feeling. Like singing telegrams, or roses with poems. It's never anonymous but she treats it like a prank each time. Even the roses. The one thing I thought she would see as a sincere declaration was the worst idea of all.

She had to leave work to go to the doctor and that was how I found out she was allergic to roses.

Jill

"You know what would be super romantic?" Miranda asks from her spot perched on my desk.

I don't ask. I already have an inkling that I'm not going to like it. Every year Miranda gets lovey-dovey around two holidays. Christmas and Valentine's Day. *Every year.* Christmas is in the rear view, but the holiday of love is right around the corner. It's on a Monday, which is perfect if you want to listen to everyone cry about it not being a federal holiday.

I don't hate Valentine's Day despite what my coworkers believe. Chocolate covered strawberries are delicious and candy in all forms should be celebrated. It's the over-the-top decorations, the wistful whining of my female coworkers, and the themed pranks Alan pulls every year that I can't stand.

Last year he sent me a singing telegram. After the one he convinced my mother to send on my birthday he must have thought the prank was worth repeating. The woman who delivered it was dressed as an anatomical heart and no amount of bribery could keep her from singing *Burning Love* to me in front of the entire office. And now the video is all over the internet.

And the women at work think it was *so* romantic.

"You and Alan should fill out the relationship declaration form," Miranda says dragging my focus away from my soup and back to her.

With a round face and large glasses, she looks a little like an owl and her tendency to perch on my desk at lunch rather than pull up a chair only adds to the comparison. Her dark skin is smooth and wrinkle free despite being almost ten years my senior which never fails to make me envious. Even as a part of human resources she fights the company dress policy at every opportunity. Dresses that lean more towards casual with their colorful designs and loose fit than business appropriate.

Today she has a satin maxi dress on with large diagonal swatches of color ranging from teal and cool blue to blood red and lemon yellow. The bow at her neck has ribbons that hang down to her waist where the dress is ruched to accent her slender hips. The scarf covering her braids is made from the same pattern. Miranda's bold style never fails to make me envious but I'm not sure I could pull off the punch of color as well as she does.

"If I've told you once, I've told you a hundred times. We are not dating," I say with a frown.

Miranda and I are work friends and maybe that's why she doesn't believe me.

"Whatever you say babe," she says dismissively waving her spoon through the air like she's shooing a fly. "Have fun with your non-relationship romance but you can only dance around each other for so long before you have to admit feelings are involved."

My glower doesn't stop her rambling. If anything, it only drives her further into her delusion.

"I played the field before I met Gerald," she says twirling her spoon through the air. "I didn't think I wanted to settle down and have a family. Thought myself a free spirit and didn't want to be trapped." She eats some of her soup and then fixes me with a stern glance. "When I met Gerald, I learned that sharing my heart with another person wasn't going to chain me down. That just because we settled down didn't mean we had to *settle*. And now I wouldn't change a thing."

We're almost at the end of our lunch break when she whips out her cell phone and begins showing me pictures of her son, Brayden, who is nine months old. Her husband, Gerald is a stay-at-home dad, and he sends her dozens of pictures every day.

"He knew I wanted to have a career and he volunteered to stay home," she told me. "But he also knows I have major mom guilt."

Scrolling through her phone I can admit that having a family is something I've always wanted. But dating isn't exactly my strong suit. I haven't gone on a date in well over a year. Even longer since I've had one turn into a relationship.

I know a family isn't going to fall into my lap and with my friends all settling down I'm feeling left behind. The pink and red heart streamers dangling from the ceiling mock me as I shove the longing down deep.

Alan

My lunch hour is spent with Michael and Henry from finance. They're good men and the only two people who know the truth at work. Everyone else thinks Jill and I are dating.

Because that's what I told them.

I fucking lied and I refuse to feel guilty about it. Eventually, Jill is going to come around and when she does it won't cause any waves at work. Pauline is on board, even if she's a little anxious that we haven't filled out the personal relationship declaration forms.

"You know, you could just ask her out," Michael says after finishing his salad.

He's a slim clean-shaven blonde with green eyes and a direct manner that contradicts his soft appearance.

"No, he can't," his boyfriend argues. "She'll think it's a prank and dismiss it off hand."

Henry is two inches shorter than Michael, with dark hair and a neatly trimmed beard and built like a tank. He looks like could be in the military with the muscle mass he carries but he is as gentle as Michael is harsh.

"He's getting nowhere as it is," Michael retorts. "Take your shot. If she rejects you, move on."

"You're such a romantic," I snark between bites of my sandwich. "Why do you put up with his shit?" I ask Henry.

"He's a fantastic lay," Henry quips and ducks out of reach when Michael tries to smack him.

"Look," Michael says leaning forward to stare at me. "Either date the woman or move on. These games you're playing are childish at best."

"Agree to disagree," I say before we pay the bill and head back to the office.

His heart is in the right place, and I know that. But he doesn't know Jill like I do. She's got her nose down to the grindstone and everything else is just a distraction. If I'm going to get her to see me, it's going to happen at the office.

My games keep me in her orbit and on her mind. And I will settle for that until I have her heart.

Jill

The last meeting of the day with Pauline and several managers to boot is where it all falls apart.

I start by going over the numbers of the Brunstein account and how according to my analysis we should change the serums we send to the store because sales are showing a downward trend.

Immediately Pauline interrupts me, "I'm sorry Jill but I'm not seeing what you're seeing. According to this report from Alan, our numbers on the vitality serum are climbing and so are our other formulas."

I freeze where I sit as all eyes turn on me. Even Chad, the doughy marketing manager famous for sleeping through these meetings is frowning at me. It takes me a moment to collect my thoughts before I can speak.

"My apologies. I must not have the right numbers for this quarter. Let me get back to you on this tomorrow." Each word scrapes my dry throat as I struggle not to cry in front of my boss.

Pauline nods and says to Alan, "Make sure she has the right numbers this time."

Like I need to have my work checked by a junior employee. Her disappointed gaze pins me to my chair until another manager takes over the meeting going over a local account.

When the meeting is over, Alan and I remain seated while everyone else files out eager to head home for the day. It's not just his successful sabotage. The effort he made to alter a forty-page document. No.

It's the shit eating grin I see when I turn to face the bastard.

"Don't worry Sweetheart. I'll make sure to give you the right numbers this time. Although if you had just asked me nicely, I would have given you the original file."

It must be the blinding rage I feel building behind my sternum that causes me to bite out, "I'm done asking you for anything Alan." My tone wiping the grin from his face.

"Is that right?" he asks with raised eyebrows.

"I'm done playing your stupid little games. You were hired with one purpose and that was to make my life easier. You are a glorified assistant. An assistant that has overstepped."

"*My* games I think you mean *our-*" he begins to say but I cut him off.

"Get on your knees." The words leave my mouth and for a second, we're both frozen. His eyes are wide in shock and I'm on the verge of apologizing and running away when he pushes back his chair. His knees hit the hardwood floor of the conference room with an audible thump.

"Don't ever correct me again," I say as he looks up at me from the floor. "The games are over. Is that clear, Mr. Landrum?"

"Yes, Sweetheart." His tone isn't apologetic, but I suspect it never is. Instead, his warm baritone washes over my skin like a caress ratcheting up the tension I feel building.

I spin to face the conference table and gather my folders while Alan remains seated on his knees at my side.

"Why are you still here?" I ask without looking at him.

"You haven't dismissed me," he says in a plain tone.

"Are you incapable of the simplest things?" I ask as I spin to face him, anger curling my words into something sharp and hostile.

"You haven't released me. The only reasonable conclusion is that you still want me on my knees for you." His words carry a hint of challenge. Ire rising even further, I can't help but glare at the bane of my irritation.

"Do *not* tell me what I want," I growl between closed teeth.

"Tell me what you want," he orders, no *pleads* with a slight hitch in his breath.

There is no reasonable explanation for the next words that come out of my mouth.

"Taste me."

I wait for him to laugh. I wait for him to derisively sneer and mock me. The laughter and mockery don't come. Instead, he slides forward to pull my thighs apart. His long fingers wrap around the tops of my thighs applying the gentlest pressure to keep me open for him as he eases his shoulders between them, his hands trailing higher.

My pencil skirt bunches around my waist as his thumb rubs me through the thin fabric of my cotton panties. A second later and my panties are tugged to the side, and I could not be more grateful that I didn't wear nylons as his tongue traces the path of his thumb.

The toes of my black pumps drag on the floor as I relax back into my chair. He doesn't waste time teasing me, we both know this tension between us has been building for a long time. His mouth is warm against my pussy as his tongue alternates between slow drags and fast licks on my clit. Before I can tell him what I like he's already switching to smooth circles around my clit, and I feel my muscles tense.

His tongue slides into my pussy as I crest the edge of pleasure. Even as my muscles clench on his tongue, Alan keeps thrusting inside me and laps my dripping arousal into his mouth. The lecherous sound of him licking me with abandon causes my breath to hitch. I press my hands against his where they are still squeezing my thighs tightly.

My skin tingles as he sucks my overstimulated clit into his mouth and swirls his tongue around it. I feel my body winding tighter and tighter as he shows me no mercy. Releasing my grip on his hands I snatch a handful of his dark hair and pull him against my pussy as I grind against his face. His tongue plunges into me as he lets me guide his face, forcing the bridge of his nose against my clit. Once, twice, and on the third I tense up and come with a moan that I bite my lip to smother.

For a moment I stay seated luxuriating in the boneless feeling leftover from my orgasms. Then I make the mistake of looking at Alan. He's still kneeling between my thighs, but his trademark smirk has a shiny coating of my arousal. The chair creaks as I sit up straight and smooth my skirt down my hips. I can feel my cheeks heating up with embarrassment as I roll my chair backwards until it hits the conference table with an audible knock.

Gaze darting to where he is still kneeling, I see his smirk his gone. Perhaps the wrongness of what just happened has hit him too. He has every right to report me to HR or to Pauline. I can't believe I let myself get so carried away that I took advantage of my coworker. He was meant to help relieve my stress but not like this. We are at work. If he doesn't report me, I will have to look this man in the eye every day knowing that he gave me two of the best orgasms in my life.

My racing thoughts slam to a stop when I feel a firm grip on my knee. Looking down I see Alan looking up at me with something that could be mistaken as genuine concern.

"Time to go home," I say around the dry lump in my throat. My voice sounds dull and raspy to my own ears, but Alan doesn't comment as he regains his feet. Cleaning his mouth with the sleeve of his dress shirt as he stands, he begins gathering his belongings.

"We have a busy day tomorrow. Make sure you get some rest, Sweetheart."

He leaves the conference room without a backward glance while I try to make sense of what just happened. Alan's tongue licked and fucked my pussy like he was starving and the pleasure he wrung from my body feels better than other partnered orgasms I've had in the past. I wonder if location played a part with the thrill of getting caught ramping the tension up.

Or if it was Alan who made it more exciting. Alan, my coworker and nemesis, the bane of my existence. The man who has made every day just a little harder than necessary. Now he has all the ammunition he needs to get me out of his way.

I'm getting sacked tomorrow. No doubt about it. Glancing at my watch I grind my spiraling thoughts to a halt. It's no use worrying about the inevitable fallout.

The stress of the day melts away as I drive home. Compartmentalizing like a pro I ignore the panic that tries to crawl up my stomach to lodge in my throat. Tomorrow is for sexual harassment meetings with HR and tonight is for enjoying the blissed out feeling following in the wake of an orgasm. A hot shower and a dinner of takeout later and I sleep like a baby through the night.

Alan

Cloud fucking nine.

I was right. She wants me as much as I want her. It's been a long road, but I finally managed it. Her eyes dark with desire and her face flushed with arousal is a sight I'm never going to forget. I wanted to take her home. To lay her down in my bed and pick up where we left off. I gave her a taste of what we can be together. I showed her how much I want to give her pleasure. When she told me to get on my knees, and I realized what she wanted, my cock got harder than granite.

It was everything I ever wanted and better than any fantasy I've had. Her taste lingers on my tongue all the way home and I savor it. I send the files as soon as I get home. I didn't linger in the conference room or at the office because I didn't want to ruin the moment.

When I step into the shower, I think of how she looked when I left. That relaxed, sated look with her bottom lip a bright red from her biting it while I brought her to orgasm.

I replay the memory as I stroke my cock. The fury and desire in her gaze as she ordered me to lick her pussy. The sweet taste of honey and the sound of her muffled moans. Coming with a moan of my own I promise myself that next time we'll come together.

Jill

When I log into my work email the next morning, I'm surprised to find the Brunstein files sitting in my inbox with an actual professional memo attached.

Jill,

I have attached the updated Brunstein files for your analysis. Please let me know if you have any questions or concerns.

At your service,

Alan

Sent almost immediately after I left work yesterday, he was prompt in correcting the error of his ways. Suspiciously he addressed me by my given name. Something he never does, in person or through email. I spend a good chunk of my allotted time to get ready for work pouring over the file, checking for red flags. I learned early on while working with Alan that if something seems too good to be true, it is a setup. When I finally dash to my closet to get dressed, I forego breakfast in favor of getting to work on time, and reluctantly admit that Alan hasn't sabotaged the file.

Probably because I could forward it to Pauline as proof that he gave me the wrong file.

One of the last to arrive at the office I'm unsurprised to find Alan, suit pressed and jaw clean shaven, sitting behind his desk tapping away at his keyboard. He was probably clocked in before the sun rose. Overachieving bastard. I am surprised to see a coffee cup emblazoned with the logo of a local coffee shop sitting on my desk next to a blueberry muffin.

"Good morning, Jill," Alan greets me with a smile. "Sleep well?"

I stare at him for a moment before taking my seat. Psychological warfare it is.

"I did. Thank you, Alan." Unable to stop at that I can't resist biting out, "Who would've thought sleep would come easier when annoying men get out of my way?"

My sarcasm seems to go right through Alan. His only reaction is that his smile stretches into a grin that highlights his dimples. Of course, the handsome bastard has dimples.

"Just let me know when I can help sleep *come* easier again," he says before turning back to his laptop.

Staring at him in silence I can't reconcile his new flirtatious manner with the sarcastic and derogatory man who has shared my office for years. My cheeks burn from his blatant double entendre.

I know it's just a new tactic to get under my skin but my knees quiver at the thought of having him lick my pussy again. I fire off an email to Pauline with my updated analysis on the Brunstein file. Glancing up at Alan I take a moment to watch him as he writes something on one of his orange sticky notes and gather my calm like an impenetrable cloak blocking out the awkwardness that is about to ensue.

"So, when are we meeting with human resources?" I ask without preamble.

"I'll message them and see when they have an opening. I'm sure they're prepped for this and will be able to see us today," he replies without looking up from his work.

"The sooner, the better," I reply, "I need to bring you up to speed on the other customer files before then."

He tilts his chin to the side before nodding in affirmation. A moment later I heard an audible ping from his computer.

"They can fit us in after lunch," he calls out and waits for my confirmation after checking our meeting calendar. He confirms the meeting via email, and I can feel the time of death for my career approaching.

I take a small sip of the coffee and I'm surprised to discover that it is a white chocolate mocha. My favorite coffee. The muffin I eat quickly because I'm hungry from having skipped breakfast. I don't care if he's celebrating his successful plan to get rid of me. It's fucking delicious.

Hours pass by quickly in the morning as I scramble to finish my reports and send them off to the appropriate departments. I have no doubt Alan can manage without me but to drop my entire workload on his shoulders while Pauline looks for my replacement would be cruel. I remember how I struggled in the years before Alan all too well.

We head to the one meeting we have scheduled before lunch, a meeting with Chad and his team to review their marketing research for the new spring product lineup.

For once Chad is alert and active in the meeting. He inserts himself into each team member's presentation to the point where every member of his staff is annoyed and aggravated.

"Thank you for your input, Chad," I say after he cuts off yet another junior member's pitch to go into a lengthy spiel about his sister's skin cancer outbreak. The pitch wasn't about sunscreen. "But I think Jamie wasn't finished pitching the rejuvenating eye cream she's been working on."

For a moment he's caught off guard. It's clear that no one on his team ever pushes back on his ego. Then a malicious smirk curves his mouth and his beady eyes lock onto me.

"You might not be aware, but I run a tight ship around here. All my reports have the right numbers at the *very* least," he chortles even as the rest of his team looks on in shame.

Fury rises from my chest but before I can find the words to dress him down and remind him that he reports to me, Alan draws his attention.

"One mistake in almost a decade," Alan begins shaking his head in disbelief. "Impressive I'll say, especially considering the mistake was due to my inability to provide the updated and corrected file. Jill has made one mistake in the lifetime of her career here at Everglow where she is a founding member of this staff. Meanwhile you're on your third strike with human resources for improper behavior and your reports are inaccurate on the off chance they are even submitted."

Chad looks shell shocked and several of his team members are hiding smiles behind their hands or looking at Alan in awe.

"I believe this is a suitable time to end this meeting. Let's reschedule this for next week on Wednesday for the same time. I look forward to everyone's uninterrupted presentations," I say holding Chad's wide eyes with my own stare. If it's the last thing I do at Everglow it will be getting him fired. "Everyone enjoy your lunch. Alan don't forget we have that meeting with HR immediately after."

"Looking forward to it, Sweetheart," Alan says as he follows me out of the meeting room.

It's only after I've shrugged on my coat and grabbed my purse that I realized Alan is waiting for me by the door.

"I was thinking about trying that new sandwich shop just down the way. Or would you prefer something heavier?" he asks.

My kneejerk reaction is to brush him off and go on my merry way to the coffee shop that makes the most delectable bear claws. But before I can summon the ire to dismiss him, I see his soft expression waiting on my opinion and I remember the way he stood up for me in the marketing meeting. Not that I needed it, but I can appreciate it.

"Sandwiches are good," I say as I wrap my scarf around my neck and lead the way out of our office and toward the elevators.

Alan

I lost my temper with Chad. I might have snapped at him even if Jill and I hadn't started officially dating. The man is on his third strike for a reason. He couldn't recognize a boundary if it slapped him in the face. And the insubordination is just a step too far.

Even when I wasn't on Team Jill, I respected her. She never asks for anything she hasn't done herself. Chad will be lucky if Jill doesn't report him to HR.

Glancing to the woman walking by my side as we make our way to my favorite lunch spot, I can't help myself.

"Are you a loan?" I watch as her eyebrows draw together at my question. "Because you have my interest.

Her mouth drops open, but no words come out. I take her silence in stride and hit her with another pickup line.

"I hope you know CPR, because you take my breath away."

She bursts into laughter, and I join her even as I rack my brain for cheesier one liners.

"Your hand looks heavy. Can I hold it for you?" I ask with a smile.

"Sure," she says before grabbing my hand and lacing our fingers together.

I didn't expect that one to land but I'm not complaining as we make our way hand in hand down the street. It's proof that yesterday wasn't a fluke. That we're on the same page and she doesn't regret giving me a chance.

We're almost to the shop when I pull her off to the side and push my luck one more time.

"Can I borrow a kiss? I promise I will give it-"

Her lips interrupt the punch line when they meet mine. Jill's fingers snake their way into my hair, destroying the hairstyle I groom to perfection every morning, but I'm not even remotely mad about it.

Our lips press and slide against each other as I wrap my arms around her waist. I have to bend down to an awkward angle but it's worth it. Her tongue slips into my mouth and the taste of the coffee I bought her this morning carries a hint of sweetness with it.

It's only when someone walking by wolf whistles that we separate.

Jill's cheeks and lips are a bright red that could be blamed on the chilly February air, but I know the truth.

We continue on our way to *O'Malley's* in silence with our hands laced tightly together and bright smiles stretching our lips.

Jill

"We are not moving in together. We haven't even had sex!" I yell in as loud a whisper as I dare from the corner booth of the sandwich shop.

With warm lighting that doesn't hurt the eyes and plenty of spacious seating, *O'Malley's* is welcoming. Clean and tastefully decorated with neutral tones, the small restaurant is better than I expected. And the tuna melt with its perfectly crisp bread on the plate in front of me is causing my mouth to water. Or it was before Alan asked me when I wanted to move into his apartment. Every other booth is filled and so are most of the tables. With so much chatter I hope our conversation won't be heard. I don't want any witnesses to this absurdity.

"Well-" he begins to argue but I shut him down quickly.

"Oral *doesn't* count!" I dismiss while smacking the table with my palm. Several people turn to look at our table, and if my cheeks weren't already on fire, I would be embarrassed enough to hide behind the table. I give them all an apologetic smile until they turn away.

"Okay. When?" he asks.

I stare at him, waiting for him to elaborate as he eats his Reuben sandwich. He finishes half before I give up waiting for an explanation he never intends to give.

"When, what?" I bite out.

"When would you like to have sex?" Alan asks earnestly.

For several seconds, my brain stalls while I try to process this auditory hallucination. Clearly this is all in my imagination. Or my dream.

"Y-You can't just ask!" I stutter out.

"Why not?" Alan asks between bites of his chips. Sea salt and vinegar potato chips, AKA the best chips in the world. His amber eyes peer into mine like he's searching for an answer and expects to find it within.

"It's not what people do," I say even as I replay our walk here. He *did* ask to hold my hand and to kiss me.

Maybe verbal consent is important to him. He's always been direct, and I don't know why I ever expected anything else when it came to sex.

"We're not people," Alan says maintaining his stare. "I have worked with you for three years and I've been in charge of your calendar for just as long. Girl's nights, trips to the nail salon, and even your doctor appointments. You schedule everything. *Everything.*"

"I'm not scheduling sex!" I shout and this time when I feel people staring at me, I do my best to ignore it. They can look at me like I'm crazy. Maybe I am. But if I'm crazy then Alan is certified psychotic.

"No? Then let's set a date," Alan says before going back to his sandwich. I watch in envy as he eats. My own sandwich still sits untouched as my stomach churns with anxiety.

"A date for what?" I ask despite the feeling of certainty that Alan has circled back to his original plan.

"For you to move in with me," he says.

"I'm not moving in with you," I retort.

Glancing at my watch I see the time running out for our lunch hour. Taking a healthy bite of my tuna I watch as a wrinkle forms between his eyebrows.

"So stubborn," he mutters. "Fine. I'll compromise and settle for a dinner date this Friday. I'll add it to your calendar."

I want to protest. Tell him I have other plans. Lie about having another date even. But the heat simmering low in my belly stops me.

Reaching over I stole some of his chips. If the man wants to live with me, he can share his potato chips at the very least. The salty goodness is wasted on his crazy ass.

I have a mouth full of chips when he adds with a devilish smirk, "I won't put it on the calendar but expect to spend the night."

The bastard is scheduling sex. Damn near demanding it. The feminist in me wants to throw hands with his presumptuous ass, but the part of me that told him to kneel on the floor and eat my pussy just wants to bend over and beg for his cock.

Compromise it is then.

"Chinese," I say holding up my index finger. "My house," I add while raising another finger. "No sex," I say with three of my fingers up.

"Pizza. Your house. Sex," Alan argues mimicking my finger count.

Just as I start to argue again Alan stops me by grabbing my hand that rests on the table. His smooth palm caresses the back of my knuckles and I'm left speechless as he looks at me with a hint of vulnerability in his gaze. The moment passes and he returns to simply holding my hand. His grip is gentle but the intensity behind his stare goes hard, removing all the softness and replacing it with a wall of cold detachment.

"If you liked my tongue, and we both know you did, you'll love my cock."

Alan

I thought the war was won. Little did I know it was merely a battle. Jill hasn't realized the depth of my affection. It's enough to have me grinding my teeth. I thought we were on the same page but at least we're reading the same book.

She let me hold her hand and kiss her. She's going to file the relationship form with human resources. We're not moving in together yet but we're making progress.

Once we've been together for a few weeks, maybe a month, I'll ask again. Preferably after I've brought her to orgasm a time or two. And if she still says no, I'll just start making practical suggestions. Leave a change of clothes and a toothbrush so the nights she spends at my apartment are more comfortable. I'll stock her favorite snacks and leave clothes at her house too. Eventually her logical brain will realize that moving in together just makes sense. If she doesn't say yes but I think she will.

I might have fallen first but I know she's not far behind now. If it costs me a few chips here or there I will survive. My Sweetheart is the only person I'll let steal my food.

But I am ordering extra chips next time.

Jill

I scheduled sex with Alan.

Technically I agreed to the dinner date. I even went as far to insist there would be no sex. He agreed but the lopsided grin on his face tells me he knows I'm lying.

All the way back to the office we walk in companiable silence. Oddly enough the little voice that should be raising hell inside my head is also quiet.

It's not until we're seated in front of the human resources manager for Everglow that I realize the meeting Alan scheduled wasn't to file a sexual harassment claim. No, Miranda already had the relationship declaration forms set out.

The entire time I panicked about getting fired and Alan was planning to declare our relationship official. There is just one problem.

"We are not dating."

"Yes, we are." Alan's no-nonsense tone is back. At lunch he was relaxed but now his shoulders are stiff, and his elbows are resting on the chair arms allowing his hands to form a loose clasp in front of his blue silk tie. He's all business and I'm left bewildered.

"No, we are not."

I might have kissed him and held his hand. But I only agreed to *one* dinner date.

"What would you like to call it?"

"Perhaps a situationship?" Miranda suggests unhelpfully. Now as she peers at me through the thick lenses of her oval glasses, I can't help but squirm in my seat. The crystal chain attached to her glasses clinks against the frame as she tilts her head at me in question.

"I don't know but we're not dating," I tell her as I cross my arms in front of me. I hear a muffled huff of breath from Alan but otherwise he doesn't interrupt.

"The company does need some kind of form filled out. Just from a legal standpoint you understand," Miranda tells me with a shark toothed smile.

She's been dying to get me to fill out this form and now that I'm sitting in her office, I know she's not going to let me leave without signing it.

"Fine. We will declare our nonexistent relationship on paper," I agree just to move this meeting along. We have work to do, and if Alan isn't going to use what happened in the conference room against me, then we need to stop wasting time in the HR office.

But my mild-mannered agreement isn't enough for him. He has to find a way to needle me, even with this.

"Legally, we are dating. Also, for future purposes we'll need a change of address form," Alan says with a wide grin stretching his lips. His perfectly white teeth on display make him look like a model for a dentistry office.

"I am not moving in with you!" I yell even as Miranda slides the form he requested across her desk. She avoids my glare and ignores my protests as Alan adds the form to his clipboard full of reports. I see her lips twitch upwards hinting at a smile, and I clutch the armrests of my chair to prevent myself from snatching the form from Alan.

"I'll need that submitted within thirty days of your move," she says even as I glower at Alan.

Miranda winking at me as we leave only adds to my irritation.

Alan

Pauline calls me into her office before I leave at the end of the day. I'm sure Miranda informed her of our visit. She's a professional no nonsense sort with her grey hair clipped into a severe bun and she wears pantsuits in every shade between grey and black with the only splash of color being her chunky necklaces. Today's selection is a canary yellow bead necklace.

"She finally agreed to go public?" she asks without preamble.

The same direct approach has steered Everglow through its first decade.

"We shouldn't see an impact on our performance. This is just a formality at this point. If anything, our interactions around the office will be less lively."

"Good," she says with a tight smile. "Because that nonsense with her laptop was a bit over the top. You both have toed the line with corporate sabotage."

"All in the name of love," I reply with a smile.

Pauline has tolerated more of our antics than I would expect from a boss. And if I didn't lie about our relationship, I'm sure she would've tolerated it less. Despite her austere appearance, she cares deeply for her employees, and much like me she is a hopeless romantic. She wouldn't be happy with my methods, particularly the lying but having Jill declare our relationship official this close to Valentine's Day makes her happy.

I'm not sure how much longer Pauling would have allowed my behavior to continue if Jill hadn't ordered me to my knees.

It's been a delicate act, flirting with Jill all these years.

She doesn't go on dates and never gossips with the other women about any of the men who work at Everglow. If she did it would have torpedoed the illusion I have steadily weaved. Her constant denial did enough damage as it was.

Jill

"Let me get this straight," Gabriella says as she sips from her glass of red wine. "He's hot as fuck, gives out orgasms like they're candy, and you want to ride his dick like it's an amusement park ride. But you don't want to date him?"

I glare at the redheaded woman lounging on my sectional. I called an emergency girl's night at my house on my way home from work and now I'm beginning to regret that decision. I've always valued her opinion but right now she's making Alan seem like a catch. Never mind all the stories I've told her through the years. She used to sympathize and help me plan my revenge schemes.

But that was before she met her husband and began trying to help my nonexistent love life. She's always been a hopeless romantic and obsessed with the holidays. Mistaking Oliver for her rideshare driver makes for the cutest story when people ask how they met. Especially when he tells his side. It was love at first sight and he claims fate and a little bit of Christmas magic brought them together just in time for the happiest day of the year. Their words, not mine.

Now my partner in crime is busy with her little family and she doesn't have time to help me plan pranks on my nemesis.

"That's an oversimplification," I say before taking a large gulp from my glass.

"No. It's really not," Gabriella argues with a pointed look over the rim of her stemless wine glass.

"Anyway," I say with a wave of my hand. I'd rather talk about anything else than my work problems.

"Just date the man," Gabriella argues immediately.

"No!"

"He wants to be exclusive and isn't shying away from commitment? In this day and age?" Emma asks with her eyebrow raised. "Marry him!"

And just like that my two best friends in the world have turned on me.

Emma and I met at a convention downtown. She was dressed head to toe in homemade chain mail made from soda can pull tabs and I was wearing a Halloween costume of my favorite videogame character Ember from *Legion X*. She was one of the few people who recognized the character by name and asked for a picture. As embarrassed as I was to have her fawn over my costume when I had bought it on clearance, I was just as enamored with her armor. The hours of dedication it took to make wowed me. We were stuck like glue for the rest of the convention and have been friends for the last five years.

"He is a condescending jackass," I say while I check on the status of our food in the delivery app. At this point I would rather watch grass grow than continue this conversation.

"Of course," Emma replies in a soothing tone. "He's a jackass who ate your pussy like a man starved."

I knew oversharing that little tidbit was going to come back to bite me in the ass. But I needed to tell someone. I just didn't think when I gushed to Emma and Gabriella that it would be used against me.

"And you already disclosed your non-relationship to human resources," Gabriella tacks on.

"Honestly it would be such a hassle to date this man," Emma replies with an eye roll.

"Such a hassle," Gabriella agrees.

Watching as they laugh and quip about my hardship brings a smile to my face. They're only pointing out the same things I've already considered.

"And really this Alan is bottom of the barrel when it comes to your potential boyfriends," Emma says as she launches into her rant about online dating. She's been trying to convince me to create a profile on the same app that she met her fiancé. "SoulConnect helped me find Andrew."

"You got lucky," I say dismissively. "You're the one percent of women who have gone out to a mountain cabin in the middle of nowhere and not become a *Law and Order* episode."

Gabriella's eyes dart around the room as she tries not to get dragged into the middle of this.

"I vetted him," Emma tells me with a frown. "I told you I took precautions. And now we're getting married."

"I am so happy for you. Really, Andrew is such a nice guy. But I don't want to try online dating. I want to meet someone organically, without all the eggplant emojis and unsolicited dick pics."

Emma nods her head in a compromising manner. Before she met Andrew, our biweekly girl's nights featured a breakdown of her best and worst matches from SoulConnect. Most notably the number of couples that messaged her looking for a third to join their relationship.

We didn't find out about Andrew until she came back from a weekend away and told us that she had met her soulmate.

Precautions my ass. She didn't tell anyone that she was meeting a random stranger whose face she had never seen for sex in a remote mountain cabin. Kinky sex at that.

When she told us about the weekend, we pressed her for details. And she did not disappoint. Honestly, I still have trouble meeting Andrew's eyes to this day, two years later.

"I didn't think you would be in town this week," I say to Emma.

She moved in with Andrew soon after that weekend and began working remotely just like he did.

"We were visiting my brother," Emma replies nonchalantly. "Andrew wants to ask him to be his best man."

"That is so sweet!" Gabriella cries from her seat on the couch.

Conversation successfully redirected to planning Emma's wedding, I breathed a sigh of relief into my glass. I love these women like sisters but I'm not ready to lie down in defeat. The pair of them are romantics at heart and they're not going to listen to my logical and sound reasoning. This is Alan we're talking about. The man who has pranked, sabotaged, and verbally sparred with me for years and would likely have continued to do so if I hadn't told him to get on his knees.

It's not my friends that Alan needs to win over. And it'll take more than fantastic sex to convince me I can trust him with my heart.

Alan

My date with Jill is an entire day away but my mind is racing. All my confidence is gone and I'm beginning to worry that I'm going to ruin what has only just begun. I let myself panic and spiral all through my dinner until I finally break and call the one person who I know will understand my predicament.

My dad answers on the second ring.

"We're dating but she's still trying to downplay our connection," I say before he can even properly greet me.

My dad is silent for a beat, no doubt collecting his thoughts before he speaks. My lack of impulse control comes from my mother. Dad is the calm in the storm that is my mother. Steady regardless of her temper. They met at work just like I met Jill. The difference being that my dad was my mom's boss at the time.

I got lucky with Jill. She isn't my supervisor despite being the person who trained me. I defer to her but there isn't any legal tape or pitfalls with our relationship. We're equals.

My parents had more obstacles to overcome than we do. But somehow, I've taken three years to get a date when it only took my mom a month.

"Give her time but also show your commitment through action. Your mother's height bothered her before we married. She was insecure that I was shorter than her and nothing I said could convince her I loved her height. Until one day I threw out every pair of shoes she owned that didn't have a heel on them."

"Mom said you tossed five hundred dollars' worth of shoes."

"I think five hundred is conservative," he says with a smile in his voice. "But it did the trick. She wore heels and towered over me for weeks. Every time she brought home a pair of tennis shoes or flats, I hid them. Until she accepted that I loved her unconditionally."

"Persistence," I say.

"Roni's my goddess but she didn't believe my words, so I showed her. Of course, now every time she misplaces a shoe, she blames me."

Jill

"A painkiller with a tall glass of water and the smell of red wine on your breath? Must have been quite the gossip sesh," Alan says as I pour myself into my chair Friday morning.

"A girl's night on a Thursday? Must have been an emergency to risk a hangover at work. Not to mention it wasn't on your calendar. I wonder what the topic up for discussion could have been?" Alan asks while looking at me with a smirk.

For the second time I notice his dimples and I hate that I notice them. Hate that he has them. As devious as he is the man shouldn't have such a cute feature.

"Shut up," I say between gulps of water.

"Did I earn their stamp of approval?" Alan asks as he brings me a second glass of water.

I want to play dumb but the earnest look on his face has me muttering the truth. As painful as it is.

"Yes."

For a blessed hour, the office is quiet. I spend most of the time catching up on emails and waiting for the aspirin to kick my headache's butt. For once in his life Alan brings me a cup of coffee that is not only hot but perfectly balanced with hazelnut creamer.

I almost checked his forehead for a fever.

By lunch I've fully recovered and I'm back to feeling like a functional human being again. Just in time for the barrage of meetings scheduled after our lunch break. Already I can feel my shoulders tensing at the mere thought of sitting in a conference room for the next four hours.

"Burgers in the park?" Alan asks when I push my chair back and stand.

I watch as he logs off his computer and straightens some papers on his desk.

"Perfect," I agree. I nearly drool as I think of a double cheeseburger with extra pickles. Greasy delicious food will even be worth Alan's dating insanity that I have no doubt he plans to subject me to.

The walk to the park is short and Alan holds my hand the entire way. Despite the lengthy line at the food truck, we get our food quickly. My double clasped greedily in my hands and Alan's bacon cheeseburger with fries in a tray he carries.

Once we spot an empty picnic table, he's quick to move the salty temptation far away from me. Perhaps I wasn't as discreet in eyeing his food as I thought.

"Don't even think about it," he says dipping a fry in a small puddle of ketchup.

I don't pretend to misunderstand.

"You want to date me?" I ask redundantly. "Share your food."

I reach for the tray, but he swiftly moves it out of my reach. I catch myself pouting and switch to a withering glare.

"If I give you some of my fries, then I'm considering this our second date," he says in his professional and clipped tone.

Despite the temptation of perfectly seasoned fries, I can't help but push back on his logic. "Tonight is going to be our first date."

"You're lucky I'm not counting that orgasm in the conference room as our first date."

I have zero doubt that my face is redder than clay and it's only the fries he finally slides my way that keep me from continuing to argue. It doesn't matter whether tonight is our first or third date. It's just semantics at this point.

We both know that unless the entire night goes off the rails then it's going to end with us naked in my bed.

Alan

It's not often that I work on personal projects during company time but it's Friday and because we're between product launches the office is quiet. All our paperwork is filed, and the marketing team is busy redesigning the spring lineup promotions. Until they have something to present our hands are idle.

So, I spend part of my day planning the perfect weekend getaway. The location is easy. It needs to be close enough to drive to but somewhere neither of us has visited. Florida overall is out. Everyone local has seen everything Florida has to offer.

I decide on Charleston, South Carolina. White, sandy beaches for me and haunted ghost tours for Jill. She's mentioned enough true crime documentaries over the years and watches too many paranormal shows not to like a ghost tour.

Not to mention the way she goes feral as Halloween approaches. Valentine's Day and Christmas she treats with apathy, perhaps even disdain. Halloween turns her into a costume critic on a sugar high from her overconsumption of candy. She goes through caramel apple suckers like each one is the last in existence.

Timing is a little tricky, but I settle for the beginning of fall. Still warm enough to swim in the ocean but beginning to hit spooky season. And far enough into the future that Jill has time to accept our relationship for what it is.

I book our bed and breakfast and add it to our calendar. A quick email to HR and our leave is approved. We'll have a long weekend together and at the end an engagement.

Jill

The night went off the rails.

It all started with our last meeting of the day. Nothing to do with the actual meeting about the Burnstein account. With the correct numbers and Alan's support it went as smoothly as possible.

No, it happened right as Pauline and the other managers were leaving. Chad came sailing through the door with a lofty smirk stretching his flabby cheeks.

"Finance cleared the expense," he says without prompting. "I've checked and the lounge is still available."

Alan and I share a confused look as we watch Pauline's shoulders sag in defeat.

"This is extremely last minute," she says in a tone that conveys her disapproval.

"Everything is approved and all we need to do is swipe the company card. My team is itching to see the Spartan's in action. Everyone will come. Even Jill and Alan will be there. Right guys?"

"Actually, we have plans-" Alan says before Chad interrupts him.

"Nonsense. This is a rare opportunity. We're talking private lounge man. And the company is covering everything."

"We won't be there," Alan says firmly. His tone goes more professional when he adds to Pauline, "It's too last minute for us."

"What a shame," Chad responds before our boss can speak. "I thought the Spartans were your team."

"They are-" Alan says before Chad cuts him off again.

"When are you going to get this chance again?" Chad asks incredulously and for once I find myself agreeing with the lout.

"We'll be there," I interject before this can drag out any longer.

The glare that Alan whips my way almost causes me to flinch.

"We can get Chinese takeout anytime. This sounds like an experience that can't be replicated. We should go," I say as the furrow between Alan's eyebrows scrunches together as he frowns at me.

"See you there," Chad throws over his shoulder as he darts out of the conference room. No doubt on his way to rope more of our coworkers into the event.

"You don't have to come," Pauline says to us but before Alan can take back my agreement, I reassure her that it's not a problem.

"We wouldn't miss it."

It's as Pauline exits the room leaving me and Alan alone that the full force of his frustration hits me with gale force.

"Our date is an experience that can't be replicated. I can watch the game from your living room if you really want to watch basketball with me."

"How expensive are lounges?"

He can't hide his wince and that settles the issue in my mind.

"We'll move our date to Saturday," I tell him and wait for his agreement.

"Fine."

"I'll meet you in the lounge."

"I can pick you up."

"If we're moving our date, I need to run a few errands. I'll meet you there."

I grip his tie and pull him forward as I raise up onto my tiptoes to press a sweet kiss to his lips.

His reluctance to reschedule our date in favor of the game only adds to his appeal. There was no doubt that he would end up in my bed tonight. But if there was, it's long gone now. And now I'm beginning to think my heart just might be ready to take a chance on him.

Alan

Fucking Chad.

Just when I think he can't be a bigger annoyance he goes above and beyond. If only he put that much effort into his actual work instead of harassing his coworkers.

A work event is *not* an ideal date by any stretch of the imagination. But the game will be over by nine and I'm sure I can take Jill out to grab a drink after. Several bars and restaurants will still be open.

Even better if her eyes are glazed over in boredom at half time, I can whisk her away sooner. Claim the experience isn't living up to my expectations. I can see a game any other Friday.

I get to the arena and the lounge early.

A few other guys are there and unfortunately one of them is Chad. I take a seat well away from him and the bastard switches seats to sit next to me. His former seatmates looked relieved at the increased distance.

The man spends a solid half hour chatting my ear off about some woman he met at the bar on Wednesday.

"Legs all the way up," he says while gesturing to his chin. "And one hell of a rack."

He's my coworker and I don't need to stir the pot. I just keep repeating that same mantra as he continues to talk to himself. Michael and Henry join us with identical eye rolls as he starts to realize I've tuned him out.

"Miranda in human resources let it drop that you're dating Sweeny. To be honest I did not see that one coming. I thought you were a man with taste," Chad says oblivious to my glare.

"You and the scarecrow? I thought that was just a rumor! Man didn't anyone ever tell you not to dip your pen in the company ink?" Chad asks while laughing at his own joke.

I watch him for a moment, letting my fury wash through me. I take a sip of my water while I wait for him to finish laughing. Almost everyone from the office is here. I can't hit him. *I can't.*

So, I stay silent even as I want to yell and smash his beer into his face. Michael and Henry watch me with disappointment in their eyes. I get it.

But they never understood playing the long game. It won me Jill. And now it will be Chad's undoing. I don't have to risk my position at Everglow or catch an assault charge in the process either. Chad's been rambling for a while, and he's spilled more secrets than he is aware of. Loose lips sink ships. And his ship is taking on water fast.

I spare a glance for the room and note that Jill still hasn't arrived. I'll give it ten more minutes and then I'm stepping out to give her a call. If she doesn't plan to attend the game, then I'll just invite myself over. I don't care if she needs to run more errands.

I'd rather be grocery shopping with my Sweetheart than here.

Jill

Rushing up to the private lounge Pauline rented for the game, I'm the last to arrive. Time got away from me while I was grocery shopping. I picked up way too many snack foods trying to guess what Alan might like. I also got him a toothbrush, shampoo, and conditioner. I don't know what brand of haircare he uses but he always smells minty, so I gave it my best shot.

Several of the woman, including Pauline are standing in a loose circle near a long table laden with snacks and drinks. I'm on my way to join them when I finish scanning the room and notice Alan seated next to Chad and a few of the men from finance. Lucy is there too, wearing a team jersey over her usual attire. It might be the first time I've seen her wear something so bright.

Almost all their focus is on the game playing out on the court below, but Chad is turned and talking to Alan instead of watching the basketball game.

"You and the scarecrow? I thought that was just a rumor! Man didn't anyone ever tell you not to dip your pen in the company ink?" Chad asks with a red face and a laugh that causes him to lean over gasping for air.

I wait for Alan to respond. To say anything, no matter how small. To admonish Chad. To put him down like he did in the marketing meeting.

But as I watch he just takes another sip of his drink and watches as the other man laughs.

The betrayal twists my stomach until I feel nauseous. Glancing around I see everyone is focused either on the game or the different conversations going on around the room. No one is looking at the door or at me.

Slipping back out of the door feels like I'm tucking my tail between my legs, but I can't confront him like this. I can't let anyone see me like this. Not until my shields are up and I can look them in the eye without the urge to cower.

It's only as I run into the women's bathroom that I realize tears are streaking down my face. I'm an ugly crier. I don't produce delicate tears that roll down my cheeks in poignant moments.

I blubber and have to blow my nose. It's ugly and it's messy.

But more than the swirling sadness that threatens to drag me under and consume a pint of ice cream and a bottle of red wine is the rage that simmers up. Rage that turns my cheeks red and dries my tears.

Alan Landrum wants to make a fool of me? Is ashamed of me?

I didn't help build a skin care company from the ground up just to be dismissed by a weak man with a thin ego and shitty taste in coffee. I am Jill fucking Sweeny and that man isn't worth the words needed to put him in his place.

Fuck him.

I thought he was different. That I was wrong about the last few years. I convinced myself that the vicious games and pranks were a shy man's attempts at flirting. My gut was right.

Alan is the condescending jackass I always knew he was. I should be grateful to Chad. Grateful that his poor attempts at locker room talk exposed Alan's true nature. I might not be the easiest person to love. But I know what I deserve, and he doesn't measure up.

He fooled me once and I fell for every line. Every touch and every kiss. He used me but I discovered the truth in time. I don't have the authority to fire him, but I can control how much influence he has within this company.

My revenge won't be swift. It'll be slow and steady. Let him think he's won me over. He won't be managing anything more important than the morning coffee order when I'm done with him.

He thought that little trick with the Brunstein account was clever. I'm going to have him twisted in knots with no clue where the sabotage is coming from while I play innocent.

Washing my face with cold water, I wait until my breathing evens out and then I reach into my purse and reapply my makeup. Eyeliner sharp enough to kill a man and mascara to make my lashes longer leaving me settled and calmed.

Inside my chest a storm rages with my heart beating against my ribs with a painful ache but on the outside, I am calm and professional. My brown eyes are warm even as my pink tinted lips tilt upwards in a cold smile.

Alan

She hasn't looked at me since she arrived. I was just getting ready to leave when she breezed through the door. Without a single acknowledgement my way she joined a bunch of women standing by the snack table.

Lucy from marketing joined those of us watching the game and I know from small talk around the office that she's in the minority who watch sports. But it soon becomes clear that she's the biggest fan in the room. It's thanks to her loud cheering that Chad finally shuts up. Seeing her in an oversized green jersey with the number '53' on the back over her normal black on black suit is almost comical.

I suspect she's timing her cheers to interrupt his sexist comments, especially considering she's usually timid and mild mannered, but I can't be sure. If she is, good for her.

He needs to be taken down a peg or two. How the man still has a job is beyond me.

"This is going to be a tight game," Henry says trying to prompt me into commenting on the score.

I grunt in agreement but I'm far more absorbed with how Jill hasn't looked my way *once*. Maybe I should have greeted her when she came into the lounge. Just because she agreed to a date with me doesn't mean I need to stop trying to earn her love.

She's locked into conversation with Pauline and a few others. The angry pinch of skin between her eyebrows is gone for a moment while they talk. As if she senses my gaze on her she looks at me and fury is back.

All my suspicions are founded. I'll make this right, but it'll need to be after the game. She might be piping mad now, but she would be embarrassed later if we cause a scene. For the same reason I didn't confront Chad I turn my attention back to the game.

Everglow is Jill's pride and joy. I'm not going to do anything to ruin that.

Jill

All through the game I can feel Alan's eyes on me. I stand with the other women except for Lucy from marketing who is a *huge* fan. Every so often she cheers loud enough to drown out Chad's incessant comments. But the rest of the women all saw this as a social networking event rather than a sport's event and for that I am immensely grateful.

I don't know if I could sit in silence with Alan and watch a game I care nothing about. I know that without the constant chatter and shop talk that I would start drowning in my own sorrow. Pity party for one please.

The bright and cheerful smiles around me remind me of why I love Everglow. It's not just the products and the salary or the student loans that I'm slowly chipping away at. It's Miranda from human resources sharing pictures of her baby and Carol from marketing pushing back on the marketing director because the color scheme is right damn it.

And it's Pauline, who has always been a friend looking at me like she knows something is wrong despite my smile.

"This isn't mandatory you know?" she says when she catches me alone at the snack table. A plate of chips and the tiniest number of carrots I can manage with a healthy amount of spinach dip.

"I know," I say between bites.

Is it so obvious that I would rather skin myself and crawl out of here as a slab of meat than endure another minute of Alan's betrayal? Probably for someone who has known me for so many years. But I tighten my resolve.

I'm *this* close to having Walter, the marketing director, dedicated to derailing the spring lineup, beaten into submission by his own team. Carol, his personal assistant, has my back and if I can convince Lucy, the marketing manager set to take over after Walter's retirement later this year, that pink isn't the devil then we will have enough votes in marketing to override Walter's decision. Lucy hasn't worn a shade lighter than grey since I've known her but now that I've seen her in the Spartan's jersey, I'm sure she'll come around to my freedom of expression speech.

"I could move Alan into distribution if it would help." Pauline's words catch me off guard and she quickly explains, "You haven't gone this long without speaking to each other since that time he switched your coffee for decaf."

"It was a really shitty thing to do," I murmur.

Nothing close to what he's done now of course. But that caffeine headache was something else. I didn't return that particular prank. He got to experience working with me decaffeinated. That was punishment enough. Plus, the silent treatment once I realized why I was on a rampage. I made cookies for everyone after that. And made sure Alan got none.

"Don't move him," I tell Pauline. "I'll sort him out. Don't you worry."

I look over to where Alan is still seated and catch his gaze. We stare at each other until the rest of the room fades to a blur. I want to make him suffer but a part of me just wants to go back in time. To walk into the room five minutes later and be blissfully unaware that my boyfriend is a traitorous jerk.

Glaring at him until he turns around to watch the game should fill me with happiness, but it just leaves a hollow feeling instead.

Alan

I hop up from my seat the moment the final buzzer sounds. The guys are high fiving because our team won, and the women just look relieved the game is over.

Nodding to Miranda and Pauline I join Jill by the snack table. She fixes her gaze on the veggie tray like she can't stand to even look at me. I know she hates carrots and right now she's choosing to stare at the orange vegetable instead of me. It's the nail in the coffin. This is something more than not greeting or approaching her. But I can't ask in front of our coworkers.

I try to think of anything I did that could upset her. I didn't have any pranks planned this week aside from that last minute switch with the Brunstein file. Then it hits me.

My lies.

The blatant and direct lies I told everyone. That's the only thing that could make her this mad at me. I can only hope she'll understand my reasoning.

I couldn't sit by at work and let another man flirt with her. Couldn't bear the thought that someone would misconstrue our games for something more malicious.

Now as she finally turns to fix me with her fiercest glare, I fight the urge to melt at her feet. It's the wrong emotion. I want her passion but not like this.

"Join me for a drink?" I ask.

"It's been a long day," she replies quickly like she didn't even consider my invitation.

"I'm going to head home then," I say before tipping her chin up with my index finger.

She might hate me, but I'm going to do everything in my power to remind her why we are a good match. A quick peck to her lips has the murderous gleam in her eye softening even if her frown still lingers.

"Goodnight, Sweetheart."

Jill

"What's wrong?" Alan asks as soon as I open my front door on Saturday night.

I thought I had played it cool yesterday but clearly not enough to throw him off my trail.

"Nothing is wrong," I reply with a sigh. "I'm just tired of marketing pushing back on the spring lineup."

Not a lie. Every spring we do the same dance at the office. Products are designed, scents are decided, promotional ads are planned, and then marketing throws a wrench into the launch at the last possible minute. Every single freaking year.

And the worst part is that it's not even Chad's fault. It's like an annual competition to see which marketing exec is going to ruin the launch.

"Walter still critiquing the color scheme?" Alan asks following me into the entryway where I have him kick off his dress shoes.

Figures the man would wear a suit to a date. An at home date at that. When he drips pizza sauce on that crisp white button down, I'm not going to even offer my stain removal spray. Let the red bleed into his shirt and stain it. Nothing less than he deserves.

"I didn't know what wine would go well with the pizza," Alan says before handing me a small potted plant. "And you have several plants at your desk so I thought you might like another to add to the collection. Figured it would be better than handing you a bunch of flowers that will die in a week."

Thoughtful bastard.

"Did anyone help you pick this out?" I ask looking at the tear-drop shaped leaves in a gorgeous blue-green shade.

"Yeah, the guy at the store said it was low maintenance," Alan says before stuffing his hands into the pockets of his slacks and rocking back onto his heels for a moment. "Do you not like it?"

"I love it," I admit before I ask my next question. "Did the man seem irritated with you?"

I watch as Alan stares at a spot on my living room floor for several moments. His eyebrows furrowed and I know the answer before he looks up to tell me that the man was indeed irritated.

"He seemed to be having a bad day," Alan says with a frown. "I was asking about buying my girlfriend a plant and he told me his wife had just left him."

"This plant," I say holding it up for his inspection. "It's called Donkey's Tail."

We stare at each other for a moment and then bit by bit we both start to crack. I dissolve into laughter first. Alan not far behind.

"He was calling you a jackass!" I shout.

"Man didn't even know me! All I wanted was a recommendation," Alan replies with a bright smile stretching his face.

"Well, you're in luck, because I don't have one of these yet," I say once I catch my breath.

Leading him through the house I show him the kitchen and then stepping out my back door I let him take in my mini greenhouse. It's not much. Just some polycarbonate sheets attached to the siding my house so that every time I step into my backyard I walk through rows of my healthy plants. The rest of the yard visible from inside the clear walls isn't very impressive. Boring grass that I have to cut every other week in the summer.

If Mr. Porter next door is to be believed I should be cutting it weekly. But that is not going to happen.

"You have more plants than the store did!" Alan's voice rings through the space and I have to muffle my laugh. "Do you swear you don't have that one? You have literally all the others I considered."

"I swear," I say with a hand to my heart. "You found the perfect plant for me."

He watches me with suspicion as I find a spot for my new plant. I'll need to repot it tomorrow but for now it can be shelved without worry. The blue pot it came in is only a little too small for its size and I have plenty of bigger planters to use. I get so swept up trying to decide which hanging pot I will use that I don't notice when Alan moves behind me.

"The one plant you didn't have?" he asks before sweeping my hair to the side. "Fate seems to be on my side."

I try to ignore the burning heat that his kisses ignite. Every lick and nibble from my throat to my shoulder where he has swept my sweater out of his way makes me want to forget his deception. At least for a night.

"You got lucky," I moan as he pulls back, his warmth leaving me abruptly.

"No, Sweetheart. I've got more than luck on my side." He takes my hand and leads me back into my house like he's the host and not the other way around. "Especially once I consider how prickly you've been this weekend."

"I have not been prickly," I protest.

"Yes, you have," he replies immediately. "There was no reason to postpone our date. The game didn't matter and there was still plenty of time after to have dinner or even catch a movie. I kept checking my phone all day just to make sure you didn't get cold feet and cancel this date too."

"Luxury lounge seemed like a once in a lifetime thing," I mutter looking away from his accusatory glare.

"If *Chad* can get Pauline and finances on board, I think I can do the same."

"I was tired," I argue and without waiting for a response because I can tell by the clenching of his jaw that he has one locked and loaded I grab my phone off the kitchen table and call in our order to the local pizza place. Three years of working together and the quarterly pizza parties ensures I know what toppings he likes.

"As I was saying," Alan says as soon as I hang up. "Prickly little cactus."

His finger playfully poking me in the collarbone is enough for me to snap.

"You!" I shout at him while jabbing my own finger into his chest. "You let that stupid man talk about me like I was a conquest!"

The anger in Alan's eyes disappears and I watch him try to piece the puzzle together of why I'm mad at him. It only makes me more furious.

"A scarecrow?" I yell poking him in the chest to punctuate every word. "Is that what the men who work at Everglow call me?"

I watch as his lips move but no sound comes out.

"Get out of my home," I say with a raspy voice. "Get the fuck out right now."

For a moment he doesn't move but then when I go to start yelling again, he holds up his hands like he's surrendering, and he leaves. Just like that and he's gone.

No words to defend himself. Because everything I thought was true. He is ashamed of me. Using me to get further in the company.

My throat feels sore and raw, and my vision is blurry from the tears. I'm almost in my bedroom when the doorbell rings.

The pizza. I know it's the delivery driver but that doesn't stop me from hoping that it's Alan. That he has an excuse or an explanation. Anything to ease this hurt in my heart.

But when I open the door, the lanky kid holding the stack of pizza boxes is the only person to greet me.

"Dude already paid," the teen says when I go to hand him the cash. "Tip too. Hope your day gets better."

The pity of a teenager is what truly sends me under. To be so pathetic that I fell for Alan and his lies is bad enough. To let him break my heart and leave it open for everyone to see is worse. Monday I will be back to myself. But it's Saturday night, I don't have to see another soul this weekend and I have three pizzas to myself. Even if one has a disgusting amount of pineapple on it.

Alan

It's so much worse than my lies to our coworkers. The ruse I orchestrated at work pales in comparison to the true betrayal.

I should've fucking hit him.

She's lost all faith in me. My sweetheart has turned bitter, and I don't know how to fix it. I never should have let him talk about her. Pauline was right there. I could've reported him on the spot, damn the scene it would cause.

If Jill heard his commentary, then I'm sure most of the others did too. I let my woman down.

Just when everything I ever dreamed to crave was within my reach, I fucked it all up. The entire drive to my apartment my mind is a tangled mess. I had so many chances to right this wrong.

At the very least I could've confronted him. Told him not to talk about my girlfriend. Insulted him. Told him Jill is a goddess he could never dream of dating. That no one of sound mind would ever choose a pathetic toad like him.

The dagger that drives it deep. If I let him feel comfortable to say these things in my company, then I'm no better than him. If he's a sexist chauvinistic pig, then so am I.

Does it even end with Jill? Lucy was there too. The only woman who felt comfortable enough to join us. Because of Chad she had to shout over him to avoid listening to his rhetoric. Just to enjoy a single basketball game. And she works in his department. How many meetings has she had to attend and listen to his comments?

When I get home, I send an email to HR. An official complaint detailing Chad's comments Friday night and his insubordinate behavior at the Thursday meeting.

It's too little too late. I know it is.

But it's a start.

Tomorrow I'll go back to Jill's house first thing. I'll get down on my knees if I have to beg her to take me back. She's the sun to my earth and I can't give up until she knows that I'll do *anything* to fix this.

The temptation to drink my blues away arises but I don't give in to it. It'll only be a bandage, it can't heal the hurt.

Sitting on my couch I replay the fight. I didn't say anything. Nothing in my defense, nothing to reassure her. I've left her crying and that is what keeps me up all night.

I have no defense and I let her down. But I shouldn't have walked away. She ordered me out of her house, but I could have stood on her porch and apologized. Begged her forgiveness.

The only thought bringing me comfort is the soft easiness we had before the fight. Jill letting me into her house and accepting my gift. Those mind melting kisses that had me forgetting the prickly behavior from the night before.

As the hours tick by my vision blurs and I'm not shocked to find myself crying. When the sky turns pink with the first hint of a sunrise, I grab my keys. It's too damn early for a Sunday but I can't wait another minute.

I gave her space. Now I need her to give me a chance.

Jill

My mope lasts until I fall asleep on my couch early Sunday morning. Everything I try to do only makes me think of Alan. In the most bizarre ways. Working together for as long as we have meant a lot of small talk. Insignificant details that I can't forget. Like how much he hated reality TV shows. I can't watch someone else's life fall apart without thinking of him. Even if the drama is one hundred percent staged.

I can't even think about touching the Hawaiian pizza still sitting on my kitchen counter. I play videogames until I fall asleep.

A loud banging sound wakes me up. Hair in disarray with several pieces sticking to my face where I've no doubt drooled in my sleep I stumble to my feet. The blanket I wrapped myself into a human burrito with tangles with my feet and nearly sends me to the ground. My knee bangs into the coffee table in front of my sofa in my hurry.

The banging resumes and I realize someone is at my front door. A quick glance at my phone shows it is only six in the morning. I consider the texts I sent Gabriella and Emma last night, pouring out my misery and realize it's one or both coming to share in my woes.

It's only after I open the door to see Alan standing on my porch that I realize I should have looked through the peep hole first. My hand goes to my messy hair automatically before I take in his rumpled appearance.

He's still in the same clothes as last night. The same suit and tie although his hair is a mess sticking up in odd directions and his tie is hanging loosely from his shirt collar which is unbuttoned. Even in a wrinkled suit he still looks better than I do. Even with red rimmed eyes he still looks like sex in a suit, and it should be enough to piss me off but all it does is send a pang of longing into my chest.

I wanted him to hurt as much as I do. And now that the damage is done, I just want to take it all back. I want to march up to him in that game and confront him on the spot. And hope that he says something that doesn't break me into pieces.

We take each other in and without a word I let him into the house. I don't need to wake any of my neighbors up at this ungodly hour on a Sunday morning by yelling at a man in my front yard.

He goes straight through my living room and back to the kitchen. I see him glance out my back door and knowing exactly what he's looking for I break the silence between us.

"I didn't throw it out," I say around a lump in my throat. "I just put it in a different pot. It was root bound."

Having a conversation with a man as hot as Alan while standing in my kitchen wearing a tank top and long basketball shorts was not part of my plan for today. I wanted to be comfortable while playing the new *Pirate's Lament* on my PlayStation last night and that meant a thin lightweight outfit that no one besides me would ever see. The top is stained with wine and paint from an abandoned project that I can't get out.

Not to mention that the guy who broke my heart and ruined my life is seeing me without a bra for the first time and my traitorous nipples are already hard.

"I didn't say anything. I wanted to but I didn't. I should have said something, anything. I just thought that if he were talking shit to me, he would leave you alone," Alan says. "It was stupid I know but I'm not ashamed of you, or of us. I've been in this one hundred percent from the beginning."

My silence only encourages him to continue.

"I'm all in, Jill. I told everyone at the office we were dating years ago. This has never been a joke to me. Not a prank. I want you to be my wife one day. I want us to date, to live together, and I want to love you." He looks down at the floor before he raises his eyes to meet mine. "I love you Jill and I have for years. I just never thought you could love me back. So, I teased you and I played office pranks on you. But always I loved you."

I can't say anything as he paces and rants across the linoleum flooring of my kitchen. The words can't scrape past my dry throat. Even if I could force them out Alan shows no intention of letting me get a word in edge wise.

"I reported Chad for sexual harassment and insubordination," Alan says with his hands on his hips as he reaches one end of the galley kitchen and spins to pace the other way. "What he said about you was completely inappropriate. He's already on his third strike and now they'll have to fire him. He should've been fired a long time ago if you ask me."

"Chad is being fired on Monday," I finally say. "It's the worst kept secret among the managers and human resources. Everyone knows."

Alan spins to face me, all the bluster he was building up gone in an instant.

"He sent a bunch of dick pics to the girls in payroll," I explain. "I think HR set a record with how fast they processed his final write up."

"Then," Alan says swallowing nervously. "I'll quit."

I start to interrupt but he waves me away, "You will never have to worry that I have an ulterior motive for having a relationship with you. You won't feel pressured to date me or worry what a breakup would do to our work."

The shine of hope is back in his eyes as he steps towards me, taking my hands in his and rubbing the backs of my hands with his thumbs.

"Just give me a chance, Jill."

"Don't call me that!" I blurt and he reels back instinctively as I surge forward to grab the lapels of his suit jacket.

"Don't *ever* call me that," I say with an intensity that shocks even me.

"Okay, Sweetheart," Alan says in that deep rumble of his. The low timber sending butterflies into flight in my stomach.

"Don't quit," I say trying to keep my voice clear even as a sob threatens to bubble up. "I should've trusted you. Trusted in myself and my heart. I love you, Alan."

"You should always trust yourself," Alan says with a smirk and a sage nod. "We both know you're always right."

"Shut up and kiss me."

And he did.

Asking him to slip out of his suit jacket had him stripping in my kitchen in a mad rush. My giggle had him glaring at me as he whipped his belt off.

"Sweetheart." His warm amber eyes meet mine in a heated blaze as he stops removing his clothes and starts working on mine.

"Kitchen table or bed?" Alan asks while leaning down to nuzzle and nibble my neck. "You have ten seconds to decide where I'm going to fuck you, or I'll lay you down on the floor."

Brain blanking as Alan follows a trail down my chest until my tank top gets in the way. I don't manage to protest until after he rips it down the middle.

"Don't pretend like you care about it," Alan growls against my chest before he begins to tease my nipples.

"Table," I moan as he nips my pebbled flesh.

"Too late," Alan croons as sinks to his knees and yanks my shorts off. "You ran out of time."

"Oh no," I simper as I sit down on the floor and lay back to let Alan slide over my body. Pants and boxers gone his warm skin feels delicious against mine.

"Mock me and I'll punish you."

"Nothing you could do to me would be a punishment."

"Tomorrow you'll get no orgasms," He breathes as he settles his shoulders under my bent knees. "Not a single damn one."

"But it's a Monday," I protest even as his tongue flicks against my clit. "Mondays *suck* and orgasms will make it so much better."

"Too damn bad you just had to be a brat," he murmurs against my slick thigh where his lips press the lightest kisses. Alan's warm tongue lapping at my sensitive flesh is ticklish and I fight the urge to squirm away. "Would've loved to call into work sick and spend the day in bed with you."

His tongue returns to my dripping core, laving me with the broad side and taking his sweet time. The slow build of heat has me thrashing but my pleas and cries are ignored. Nothing I can do speeds up his movements, the infuriating pace is steady as I fall into madness.

And just when I'm on the edge and about to plunge into ecstasy, Alan pulls back and covers the length of my body with his own.

The sharpness of his smile has returned, and I know that I won't be making any demands in our bed for a long time to come.

"I promised myself that the next time we would come together," he says with a gleam in his eye.

Notching his head against my core he leans forward to kiss me as he slides the entire length of his cock deep into me. Alan groans against my lips as my heat grips him. With his cock fully seated I can't help but to grip his shoulders and wiggle my hips against his in a wordless plea to move.

"I never want to stop fucking you," he growls into my ear as he curls above me, his thrusts slow and steady in the same beat as his licks from before.

"I'll remember that tomorrow," I say arching my breasts into his mouth. His tongue flicks over my nipple as his mouth sucks the tip.

"Not even if you beg me," I barely hear him say as my body shudders as my climax sweeps over me like a warm wave of water. Pleasure seeps from every inch of skin but in the aftermath Alan's strokes have gained speed and I'm rapidly approaching the edge of ecstasy again as the hard length of his cock rubs against my inner walls. The aftershocks of my orgasm causing my muscles to clench him as his dark eyes catch mine. The molten amber pools pouring his soul into mine as every second slows down and I can soak in every ounce of love I see there. How I didn't see his own affection when it so closely mirrors mine, I'll never know.

Screaming his name and scratching my nails down his back as he seizes above me, I fill his warmth feel me as the last dregs of my orgasm milk him for every drop of his come.

We lay in a melted heap of body parts as we catch our breath and allow our bodies to cool.

"How are your knees?" I ask after a while, wincing at the thought of his knees and the damage my kitchen floor surely did to them.

"Keep being a brat and it'll be you on your knees," Alan retorts immediately with a playful pat to my hip. "On a serious note, next time the floor is off limits. Unless there is a very plush rug."

Alan spent the night and left early in the morning to get ready for work. But not before dragging me out of bed and pouring us both bowls of cereal. He told me over our breakfast that he thought about packing an overnight bag on Saturday night but didn't want to be presumptuous.

Sitting at my tiny kitchen table in nothing but his white undershirt and boxers as he spoons mouthfuls of cinnamon toast crunch into his mouth feels domestic. Like everything else doesn't matter so long as we are together.

"Next time," I say.

"We talking airline carry on size or personal item?" he asks with a smirk knowing damn well he could carry a full set of luggage through my front door, and I would let him.

"Use your intuition," I say before tipping the bowl back and drinking the leftover milk.

The kiss that follows curls my toes and lights my soul on fire. I'm three seconds away from crawling in his lap when he pulls back and taps my nose.

"Remember our little talk last night?" he asks with a crooked grin. "No orgasms for you."

Luckily, he had to leave right away to make it back to his apartment or else we both would have been late. Because if he hadn't left, I would have tied him to the bed until we were both boneless and satisfied.

Alan

I get to work early to make sure I could stop by human resources before Chad's termination. Miranda arrives, and I quickly wave her down to get the form I need. The email would get the ball rolling and an investigation started but I want to fill out an official report of sexual harassment. I make sure to include all the details as Miranda watches me with amusement in her eyes.

"He's already being fired," she says.

"I know, but I want it on record," I reply while checking my phone to get the exact date of the meeting.

"The king of harassment filling a harassment report?" Miranda asks.

"King of harassment?" I ask.

"Jill made you out to be a devil," Miranda croons.

"If Jill ever asked me to stop I would. Instead, she sinks to my level and gives as good as she gets."

And she holds me accountable. I'm not a good man, but I will be better. There are too many occurrences of Chad's behavior that I should've reported. Enough of the women have stepped forward to have him face disciplinary action but he should have been fired years ago.

That scarecrow comment didn't appear out of thin air.

I grab Michael and Henry on their way in to work, pulling them into an empty conference room. My friendship with both men has flourished through the years making our work relationship that much smoother. It's rare that I have to pull rank.

"Chad is being fired today," I immediately say.

"We know," Henry says after he and Michael share a look with each other.

"I am the only man who filed a report against him," I tell them.

The only response they give me is a pair of raised eyebrows from Henry and a puzzled frown from Michael.

"For those comments about Jill?" Henry finally asks.

"Yes," I reply. "But every man in this office has heard his comments about the women who work here. We've seen him harass them day in and day out."

Henry connects the dots before Michael. A sharp glint entering his brown eyes.

"You're holding us accountable." It's not a question.

"Going forward," I say nodding. "I'm going to help Miranda set up a presentation on workplace harassment next week. I'll also talk to Lucy and Walter so that we show a united front in the meeting. From now on I want it to be clear that we are all accountable for making this a safe work environment."

"See something, hear something, say something," Michael mutters to himself raking his hand through his hair.

"Exactly," I agree.

Henry frowns crossing his arms in front of his chest.

"I encouraged Flora and Ashley to report him when I heard he sent them dick pictures. I shouldn't have left it at that. Should've reported him myself."

I clap him on the shoulder. He understands where we all went wrong. It clearly unsettles him as much as it does me.

"Going forward, we'll do better," I say before I leave them in the conference room.

I've worked in Jill's shadow for the last three years. She laid every piece of groundwork, finding the best way forward, and essentially handed me a road map. Now I finally feel like I'm bringing something new to the table. I can't change the past, but we can learn from it.

And I'm going to lead us into the future.

Jill

"I filled out the change of address form," I say as I walk into work.

Alan looks up from his computer. His eyes are tinted pink and there are visible bags underneath them. Despite our talk and the night we spent together, the strain of our fight still shows. But I expected this. Alan keeps his walls high but once they come down, he's immensely vulnerable.

Knowing that I hold the power to crush him, to break his heart leaves me breathless. But seeing his soft and squishy emotions reassures me that I can trust him with my own feelings. That I can trust him with every part of me. And he needs to know that I do trust him.

His deep amber eyes shine with love as he looks at me, and I begin to ramble. The words rushing out of my mouth like the faster I speak the quicker he will return to his confident and self-assured self. A grown man who can handle my demands and roll with my verbal punches.

"For you, obviously. I am not moving into an apartment when I have a perfectly good house with a ridiculously good interest rate on my mortgage."

He slowly pushes his chair back and stands as I continue my rant.

"Once we're married, I'll add you to the deed," I say as his large hands come up to cup my heated cheeks. My own hands smooth down his suit lapel, stroking the soft fabric right over his heart.

His eyes are dark with emotion as he finally breaks his silence.

"Oh? Now we're getting married?" His deep voice carries through the office, but I'm not worried about the whispers from our coworkers or the eyes I'm sure are watching everything unfold from every direction.

"By your logic we've been dating for three years already. I'm not waiting until year seven for a ring, Alan." A light smack to his chest accompanies my words. Like a stamp of approval on a work expense. My light tone belays the nervous twist in my stomach. That my proposal is too much too fast.

"Never thought I would get engaged on Valentine's Day. Look at you being romantic," Alan says teasingly.

The smile that stretches his lips is joyful and bright as he leans down to kiss me. My vision goes blurry as his lips meet mine. I hear clapping but it's muffled by Alan's hands that are woven into my hair. I don't care that we're in the office or that our coworkers are staring. They all thought we were together years ago.

"Understood," Alan says when we part to catch our breath. His voice is lighter than normal as he catches his breath. "Do you need me to submit that form to HR?"

"I've got it," I say with a smile. His own smile is back in full force, reaching his eyes and as always, he looks as neat as a hairpin. Except for his blue striped tie, which my wandering hands clearly found while we were kissing. Straightening his tie, I fiddle with it for a moment longer than necessary.

Another chaste kiss and I turn to go back to my own desk. "And Alan?" I call over my shoulder.

"Yes, Sweetheart?"

I take a moment to relish the nickname that I once found so demeaning. Now I know it was his way of claiming me all those years ago.

"Happy Valentine's Day," I say with a grin.

A week ago, I wouldn't have imagined myself engaged. And on the day of love itself no less. Already I can practically hear Miranda's squeals of joy. And Gabriella and Emma's gloating.

"Happy Valentine's Day, Sweetheart," he says before turning back to his desk, because we are at work after all and we're nothing if not professional. My proposal being an obvious exception.

I texted the group chat before I walked into work, and I can feel my phone vibrating in my purse. I'm sure that they are blowing my phone up with a million questions. Last they heard Alan was a rat bastard who was going to die in a trap befitting a rodent. I'm sure I gave them whiplash between Friday night and today, but I know in my heart that this is the right choice.

It took a long time to get here but now I know I'm right where I need to be.

My first task of the day is firing off an official email letting Miranda know that she can file that form. It's only after I click send that I realize I've fallen for one more of Alan's pranks.

He changed my email signature to read Jill Landrum instead of Jill Sweeny.

"Seriously?" I ask looking around my laptop to meet his amber eyes. He approaches my desk in a casual stroll with his hands tucked into the pockets of his slacks.

"You beat me to it," he says with a grin. "But I didn't want to ruin my surprise."

And then in front of everyone he pulls a black velvet box out of his pocket and sinks down to one knee beside me.

"I know you already made your demands, but will you, Jill Sweeny, do me the honor of marrying me?" he asks with a cheeky grin.

"Yes," I say with tears in my eyes. "But that is seriously the last time you're allowed to call me by my name."

"Deal, Sweetheart," he says before pressing a gentle kiss to my lips.

Epilogue

Jill

"They will love you. I swear," Alan whispers with his cheek pressed against my head and his arms wrapped around me from behind. "How could they not love the woman I love?"

He is so sure of his parents' approval. So confident and cocky and I'm a bundle of nerves.

"We got engaged before I met them," I mutter in protest.

"Worried my father won't give you my hand in marriage?" His attempt at a joke makes me laugh but the nervous energy doesn't abate even as I picture Alan in a Victorian era dress accepting suitors.

"We had a very tense work environment for many years. Are you sure you never spoke badly about anything I did to you?"

"Well," he begins with an audible sigh. "Yes I suppose I did."

"What did you tell them?" I turn on him in a flash. "I need to know so I can tell them my side."

"It's all water under the bridge," he tries to dismiss my worry, but I'm hooked like a fish on a line.

"Jello stapler?" I ask as he grabs our bags from the back of the rental car. "That time I convinced you we were wearing Halloween costumes to work? Or was it when I programmed your email to send all company emails into the spam folder?"

My anxiety builds as I consider every single prank I've ever pulled. Every clever move in our chess game comes back to haunt me as I view it from an outsider's perspective. They're going to see me as their treasured son's bully. Worse, they may view our relationship as a power imbalance.

"Jill," Alan says with a hint of exasperation coloring his tone. "I told them about you changing my email signature to read '*Adam Longhorn*' and how I didn't notice for an entire week. My dad still laughs whenever my mom brings it up. Which is every time I don't notice something new, she's done around the house."

"Oh, that's very mild for us."

"Exactly," he says grabbing my hand and leading me towards the front door of the cabin we're sharing with his parents for the week on the shore of Lake Allatoona. "But please don't tell them how I retaliated."

"Alan Landrum, do you want me to lie to your mother?"

"No, just don't volunteer it."

"But she needs to know what a monster her son has become."

"No, she doesn't. I'm an angel and it's staying that way, Sweetheart."

"We'll see." Already the wheels are turning inside my head with ways to steer the conversation. I could comment on her curtains, letting her know that Alan told me she had just replaced the linens last month. Something his father made sure to tell him.

"Sweetheart." Alan's deep timber causes goosebumps to rise along my arms and neck. "Don't you dare."

I don't reply. I just give him a wide smile with the biggest and most innocent doe eyes I can manage. He doesn't buy into it for a second but that's the point. He knows I'm going to leverage this against him. I'll paint him the villain in front of his own family and watch as their idealized version of him burns to a crisp before their very eyes.

But even as we reach the porch and ring the doorbell, I know this is all going according to his plan. Distracting me with a good-natured sabotage plot is exactly what I needed to settle my nerves. Alan knows me better than anyone else.

"Alan and Jill are here, Roni!" a man with salt and pepper hair clipped close to his scalp hollers over his shoulder as he answers the door. He's like an older version of his son in a white button down and khaki slacks.

He's shorter than Alan with a slightly rounded belly but the same warm smile stretching into a grin as he pulls my fiancé in for a hug.

Before I can say hello, a tall woman darts around the pair and swoops down to latch her arms around me. I'm spun in three circles before she releases me.

"Finally, we get to meet you!" Alan's mother, Roni shouts with a wide smile. Her curly messy hair is at odds with her son's meticulously styled and groomed appearance. Dozens of bangles slide along her forearms and a large gemstone necklace hangs down the front of her bohemian dress.

"Hi, Roni. Can I call you Roni?" I ask as she peers down at me with the same warm amber eyes that I've grown used to loving. She's several inches taller than her son even in her flat tan sandals.

"For now, darling." She tugs me into the cabin as she leans down to whisper in my ear, "I hope in time you'll feel comfortable calling me Mom."

The lump in my throat swells unexpectedly as my vision blurs and I have to take a moment to push down the warm squishy feelings her words have brought to the surface.

"Maybe after we're married," I reply as we breeze through the cabin and Roni shows us to our bedroom, letting us settle in before we all regroup in the kitchen later.

"Of course, we've only just met," Roni says before she leaves us to get settled. "I just feel like I know you so well. Al has talked about you for *years*. Without fail he managed to bring you up at every holiday and family dinner. He had it *bad*."

"Years?" I ask as I watch Alan try to hide a wince. "Al?"

"Don't you dare," he growls pointing a finger at me sharply. "She's my mother and I have to tolerate her nicknames."

"Sounds familiar, *Sweetheart*," I say placing a light hand on his linen shirt sleeve.

"It's no secret that I take after my mother," he says with an eyeroll. "Don't even think of calling me-"

"Calling you what?" I interrupt him. "A mama's boy?"

He turns to me with a mocking expression. With a quick flick of his fingers his shirt collar is unbuttoned. Next go his cufflinks.

"You're such a fucking brat."

"No stop! It tickles," I cry as his hands go to my waist. He pins me down with his body weight as he drags the tips of his fingernails down my curves.

"Quiet now, Sweetheart," he breathes against the crook of my neck. The heat of his breath against my cool skin sends shivers down my spine raising goosebumps along my arms and neck. "Wouldn't want my parents to hear us. Would you?"

"Ugh," I complain pushing against his shoulders. "Moment ruined."

"Next time I'm not stopping because of your delicate sensibilities. So, you better behave."

"You better behave, or you'll be on your knees making me come twice before I let you even think about touching your cock."

"There is my bossy babe," he says before leaning in for a slow languid kiss. "I missed her."

"We need to join your parents."

"If you insist." He sighs before leaving me on the bed to change his clothing into something more casual for the lake. "Heads up but my parents are a bit more affectionate than most people would define as appropriate."

"I was kind of picking up a hippie vibe from your mom."

"Yes. Just don't call her a hippie to her face. She hates the term."

Alan grabs a pair of swimming trunks with a palm tree pattern while I consider which of the swimsuits I packed for the trip I want to wear. The black one piece does wonders for my curves but the bikini with the underwire support makes my breasts look fantastic. I almost decide to play it safe and go with the one piece but considering what I know about his parents I go with the bikini. It covers just as much of my bobbles and bits as the other, it just exposes my soft stomach.

"Are you sure you want to go swimming?" Alan asks me once I ask him to help me tie my top in place. "We could have so much more fun if we just stay in the room."

"This is a *family* vacation," I grumble. I wave the loose strings over my shoulder in a hurry up gesture and wait for him to begin tying the ends together before I add, "Save it for our honeymoon."

"We need to start planning the wedding."

"It sounds like so much work, honestly."

"I'll make lists and appointments. You just pick what you like, and I'll take care of scheduling."

"You'll do all that?"

"Well, yes. It's just a big party, right? We've thrown dozens of those. This will just be fancier and more expensive. I can offer design advice and mail invitations all day."

"I love you."

"Love you too, Sweetheart."

A moment later I feel a tugging at the strings holding my bottoms in place.

"Alan, are you undoing my swimsuit?"

"Sorry, not sorry," Alan says undoing the string holding my top in place. "I promise I tried to resist."

Soft lips caress my skin, trailing their way up my shoulder to my neck and up to my ear.

"I just started thinking of you in a white dress, putting on this act like you're a good girl and how much I'm going to enjoy taking it off you and making you beg for your husband's cock."

It was a long time before we went swimming.

The End

Check out Pumpkin Spiced Love to read how Emma and Andrew met through the SoulConnect app for kinky sex and found their soulmates. It's nonstop spice centering around Halloween with the fall festival in Crescent Ridge making a special appearance.

Pumpkin Spiced Love

Jacqueline Carmine

Content Warnings

Graphic Sexual Content
Bondage
Unprotected Sex
Breeding Kink
Primal Play
Mask Kink
Religious Role Play (Priest/Nun)
Breath Play
Verbal Degradation (Whore/Slut Etc.)
Spanking (Mentioned)
Grave Desecration

Emma

"Shut the fuck up and take that dick like a good girl," Andrew breathes against the arch of my neck right before he leans back to look at where his cock is pounding into me. The first words he has ever spoken to me make me impossibly wetter as he continues his invasion of my body. His tattooed hand leaves my breast and wraps around the hollow of my throat. A warm choker of roses and thorns.

"My hand looks so good around your neck baby girl," he says with a firm squeeze.

Warmth spreads through my core as he applies pressure to my throat at the same time as he begins rubbing my clit in smooth fast circles.

"I'm so close," I whimper when he lets go of my neck to grab my thigh and lift it high on his hip. "Don't stop. Please God don't stop."

His eyes hold a feral gleam behind the mask's eye cutouts. The blue eyes stand out from the white mask in the shape of a shocked ghost. He had answered the door silently and naked except for the mask just as we had agreed on the app. If I had known the things he would say I never would have chained his voice for even a moment.

"I'll never let you go now," he promises in a raspy voice. Beads of sweat roll down his chest and I feel the bizarre urge to trace their path with my tongue.

"Mark me," I order as he resumes circling my clit.

His hips begin to stutter when I go over the edge arching my back and thrusting my breasts forward. He jerks back pulling his cock out while my walls are still spasming with the aftershocks of my orgasm. He strokes his cock as he paints my belly and mound with thick ropes of his seed. For just a moment I regret not asking him to come inside me. I'm on birth control and we've both been tested. It was something we discussed before I even bought my plane ticket.

Andrew sits back on his heels as we both take a moment to catch our breath.

Downloading the SoulConnect app on my phone was a whim. Sharing all my kinks that I was too embarrassed to tell any previous boyfriend about with a stranger was easy. Meeting a stranger to have sex and fulfill those desires was crazy and scary. Coming to his cabin in the mountains without vetting him was foolish. He could be a serial killer ready to carve me up and feed me to the local wolves. A little risk and danger had set the perfect mood for my mask kink.

"Cool if I take this off now?" Andrew asks.

I nod and watch as he pulls the rubber mask off his sweaty face. His dark hair falls in loose damp curls over his ears, and he has a scattering of freckles over his nose. His blue eyes meet mine and it feels like my breath is knocked out of me.

I need to leave before I beg him to kiss me. We had consented to a single encounter with no strings. It is time for me to go.

As I begin to gather my things Andrew watches me with a sheepish expression. Just as I slip back into my dress, he finally breaks the silence.

"Feel free to say no but would you like to get breakfast with me?" he asks as he grabs his dark wash jeans and pulls them on.

He's not looking at me and for a moment I fear it's a pity invite but then I see his Adam's apple bobbing nervously as he waits for my answer.

"I'd love some waffles," I say with a shy smile.

I've always been the safe bet. The girl the parents like and invite to holidays but never the woman who ignites a man's darkest desires. Plain boring and vanilla until Andrew and I clicked together on the dating app.

Now I'm going to have breakfast with a man whose face I didn't see until *after* we had sex. A man who readily agreed to wear a mask and choke me while he fucked me.

"There's a little diner up the road. Looks awful but the food is phenomenal," Andrew says as he slips a T-shirt over his head and grabs a pair of black framed glasses off the side table.

"I'm not local so I'll take your word for it," I tell him as he leads me outside his cabin. I go to hop in my car, but he stops me with a hand on my arm.

"Unless that's all-wheel drive you might want to ride with me," he says gesturing at his old square bodied truck.

My hesitancy to leave my car behind is telling and he's quick to explain.

"It's a little way up the mountain on the ridge. There is a small town there and the road isn't paved and we're expecting rain. You can take your car but if it gets stuck, I'll have to bring you down in my truck and then you'll have to wait for a tow truck. I don't have the equipment to pull you out of the mud much less tow you down the mountain," he says rubbing the back of his neck.

I appreciate the explanation, but the car is a level of security I need. Knowing I can leave at any time if I'm uncomfortable or don't feel safe isn't a luxury I want to give up.

"I'll follow you up and I'll be careful," I tell him before I climb into the driver seat of my rental car.

He waits for me to get settled and then he closes the door for me. It's a little bit more than just up the road but when we pull into a gravel parking lot beside a rundown little shack of a diner my stomach is rumbling and I'm ready for food.

He opens my door and holds my hand as we enter the diner.

"Morning Andrew," a woman old enough to be my grandmother greets him before the door closes behind us.

"Hello Wendy. Tobias. This is Emma," He calls over to the counter where she is ringing up a large man in a flannel shirt and dirty jeans.

They both turn to look at me and I give a little wave as Andrew leads me to a booth by the windows.

"Small town," he says before I can ask.

Coming from a city where I can never be alone outside my apartment but surrounded by strangers, I feel a sense of longing. To know everyone and have everyone know me.

"Finally use that mail order bride website the men were telling you about huh?" Wendy asks when she comes over to take our order.

"No!" Andrew immediately shouts. "She's just my date, not my wife."

His face is flushed red in embarrassment. The woman and I share a look before I order a stack of waffles and sweet tea. Andrew orders an omelet and coffee.

"So, mail order bride?" I ask when she walks away.

"Small town. No, tiny town," he says rubbing his temples and avoiding my gaze. "Few women live up here and it's difficult to meet anyone when you work for a logging company or live off grid. A lot of the mountain men around here have to send off for wives just to have a chance at love."

"But not you," I reply.

"I'm not marrying a stranger," he replies as Wendy brings our food over. She's gone in a blink without a word and when I'm sure she's out of earshot I can't help but tease him.

"Worried you'll end up married to an axe murderer?"

"No. I'm worried she'll take one look at a man like Tobias and trade up," he replies between bites.

"Tobias seemed nice," I say.

"He doesn't know what STFUATTDLAGG means," Andrew says dismissively.

"I'm sure I could teach him," I say needling him a bit further. Jealousy has never been a turn on, but the possessiveness Andrew is displaying has me squirming in my seat and rubbing my thighs together.

"Stop it before I spank you in front of everyone," he orders locking his blue eyes with mine.

A part of me wants to continue and see if he is bluffing but another part just wants to drag him back to bed for round two.

"Have I been a bad girl?" I ask just as he takes a bite of his omelet.

Watching him choke shouldn't be a turn on, but it is when I'm the reason he forgot how to swallow.

"I guess you'll just have to punish me after breakfast," I add playing with the strap of my dress as he chugs his coffee.

"You little brat," he growls as I turn my attention to my waffles.

They are thick and coated with a heavy layer of butter on top. I pour a thick maple syrup over them until it drips down the sides of the stack and pools on the plate. As Andrew devours his omelet, I take small, measured bites of sweet fluffy heaven.

He watches me over the rim of the coffee mug emblazoned with the diner's logo as I slowly work my way through the stack. Rain begins pelting the diner's windows and the blue sky has gone grey.

"You can try to drag this out all you want but you're still going to be punished when we get home," he mutters as I finish up.

"It's called table manners," I reply with a raised eyebrow as I place my knife and fork in a cross on my plate.

I try to split the check, but he waves me off when I go for my wallet. Wendy tosses me a wink as we leave and shouts, "Look forward to seeing you around the ridge, Emma!" before the door closes behind us.

I smile and catch her eye through the glass door. I wave goodbye before we dash through the heavy rain to my car.

"I'll lead you down. Keep my taillights in view and if you lose visibility stop. More than one person has gone over the edge of the mountain in the rain," Andrew says as he opens my door so I can slide into my car.

I nod unable to vocalize my thoughts in any kind of coherent manner. I want this to be more than teasing. I want to continue flirting with this kind and chivalrous man.

Following him back to his house is slower with my windshield wipers barely able to keep up with the rain. More than once I follow him to ride the middle of the gravel road when deep ruts have filled with muddy water on the sides of the road. We passed no one on our way down and when we reached his cabin, I breathed a sigh of relief. I thought he was exaggerating but I had peaked over the guard rail as we drove down, and the steep drop coupled with my car's poor traction had stolen my breath.

Climbing out of my car before Andrew could make his way over to me, I ran to the front porch. Heavy steps pound against the wet ground right behind me and I whirl around as I reach the front door only for him to pick me up by my waist and pin me to the mahogany door.

His mouth slams against mine and all I can feel is the smooth glide of his wet skin on mine. I grab twin handfuls of his hair even as my legs wrap around his waist, my thighs squeezing him as tight as they can. Fighting to get closer I wiggle until I can feel his cock pressed to the warm heat between my legs. The rough denim brushing against the thin gusset of my panties.

He thrusts his hips at the same time as his tongue enters my mouth. Rough and solid, his kiss sets me alight with fiery passion. He breaks our kiss to latch onto my neck and I moan as warm tingles spread from where his teeth drag against the sensitive arch to the tips of my breasts.

"Hold on," Andrew orders as he shifts my weight to his left hand and frees his other to open the door. Lingering heat from this morning eases the chill from the rain as he carries us into the cabin slamming the door behind us.

Clutching his firm shoulders, I cling to him as his long strides carry us through the house. I reach down his back to grab the hem of his shirt and begin pulling it up over his head as we enter the bedroom.

He bumps the dresser when I whip the shirt over his head, and he chuckles at my eagerness. It's only been a few hours since we had sex, but this feels urgent. The teasing has built up tension that only Andrew can ease.

I drag my nails down his smooth chest as our lips press together soft and solid at once. Stumbling towards the bed he lets me pull him down, never breaking our kiss. I wiggle to line up our hips even as he grinds down to meet me.

Pulling back for a moment, Andrew shoves the top of my dress down to bare my breasts and I slip the straps off my arms to help him. Mouth latching onto one peaked nipple he thrusts against my core as I moan. Nails scratching his scalp and back, anywhere I can get a grip all I can do is lay back and claw as he drags a rough tongue against my sensitive nipple. His free hand captures its twin rubbing a callous thumb against the nub as his tongue swirls around the other.

"Andrew, stop teasing," I cry as the heat between my legs continues to rise. I can feel my arousal spreading. My panties are damp and likely my dress as well.

I feel his chuckle before I hear it.

"Only good girls get to come on my cock," he says after releasing my nipple with a pop.

"No," I beg as he switches sides. Warmth pools low in my belly and my legs tingle as he continues to play with my nipples, teasing me higher and higher until I plunge off the cliff in a wave of ecstasy.

My pussy clenches on air and I moan at the lack of his cock, his fingers, *anything* to fill it.

Not all orgasms are created equal and if he doesn't get his cock into me before the next one, I might just become the axe murderer I feared meeting in the mountains.

"Andrew," I growl after he palms both of my breasts and squishes them together. He alternates licking one hardened peak and then the other.

"You don't give the orders in this bed, Emma," Andrew says before he lets go of my breasts and slides off the bed to kneel between my legs. My hands grip the bed spread as he palms my thighs spreading my legs wide to accommodate the broad expanse of his shoulders.

He pushes the skirt of my dress up until the entire garment is bunched around my waist. My blue panties slide down my legs and just when I think he's going to remove his jeans and give me what I've damn near begged for his tongue flicks my clit.

Warm wet tongue tracing my slit he meanders for a bit before thrusting his tongue inside me as far as it will go. Plunging deep and stroking my walls his grip on my thighs is sure to leave bruises even as his tongue paints me. When he does remove his tongue, I'm a quivering mess on the edge of a second orgasm and when he turns his attention back to my clit I shake and moan as I crest the edge again.

But he doesn't stop there. He gives me no quarter as his tongue laps at my clit. He doesn't let me move even as I instinctively try to wiggle away from the contact on my oversensitive nub. Lips latch onto my clit forming a tight seal and as he sucks on the tight bud it's everything I can do not to scream.

"I-I need you," I moan as my hips flex against his hold, back arching and teeth grinding as electricity runs down my veins. My heartbeat is loud in my ears, and I don't hear his response as he finally relinquishes his hold.

I watch in a daze as he unbuttons his jeans and slides the denim and his boxers off in one go. His gaze is hungry, and

I can't look away from the intensity. He looks at me like he knows every part of me. This has turned into far more than a hookup for either of us.

As he crawls back onto the bed, I reach for him, and he comes readily into my arms. Our kiss is messy in the best ways. I taste my arousal on his lips and tongue as he lines up the head of his cock with my entrance.

"Guess I'm a good girl now," I mumble as he slides inside of me.

"So, fucking good," he growls thrusting slowly. "A good girl who knows just how to take me."

"Like this?" I ask with a mumble as I squeeze my muscles around his girth. His eyes go wide with shock, and I can't help the giggle that bubbles up.

"You're gonna pay, Emma." He slams into me brushing my clit with his pelvic bone. Again, and again his hips slam against mine pushing us up the bed with the force.

Just as I go to ask if he prefers cash or a card his hand covers my mouth squeezing my lips together.

"Mpmh." Is all I can get out around his palm. His blue eyes sparkle with mirth even as his eyebrows create a furrow on his forehead. Grumpy but playful.

"Look at you." He leans back to look at where our bodies are joined. "You look so good when you're sucking my cock inside of you."

Bending over me changes his angle and suddenly the head of his cock is hitting the perfect spot making me gasp beneath his palm. Breathless I almost don't hear his next words.

"It's like you were made for me," he whispers into my ear, and I come, screaming against his hand. I feel him pull out at the last second bathing me in his seed again as my joints stiffen and lock as my vision goes dark.

I wake moments or minutes later underneath the covers sprawled across Andrew's bare chest.

"There you are," he says fondly realizing I'm awake. "How was your nap?"

A slap to his chest just makes it rumble with laughter under my head.

"My car is stuck," I announce without a hint of guile.

"You haven't checked-" Andrew begins to brush me off when he stops midsentence realization hitting him and making his blue eyes shine bright with hope. "Oh."

"Oh," I repeat with a nod.

"You'll stay the weekend?" Andrew asks.

"If that's okay," I reply. "I can reschedule my flight."

"More than okay," he replies pulling me in for a kiss. "It's perfect."

It's impulsive and crazy but I'm done playing it safe. You'll never hit a home run sitting on the bench and I've finally found something worth stepping up to the plate. His eyes grab my attention when we separate, the pupils dilated to the point that they're beginning to swallow the blue.

"Do we-" He stops. "Can we-" he attempts before shaking his head.

I wait for him to gather his thoughts.

"Delete our profiles?" he asks after a moment.

"Well, I don't know about you, but I don't want other women messaging my boyfriend trying to hook up with him."

"A yes would suffice."

"Too boring."

"Such a brat," he says before swatting my ass.

The slight sting reminds me that he still hasn't made good on his threat.

"You never did give me that spanking."

Andrew

I knew it before I took her to *Lenny's*. Emma is perfect. Not literally. She's a normal human woman with quirks and imperfections. To anyone else looking in this would look like a fleeting infatuation. But in a very palpable and tangible way I know she's mine. This is more than a crush or a fling. This is my forever, and I need to handle this with care, or I will ruin the best thing that's ever happened to me.

I need to play it cool.

"Want to go to the Halloween festival later?" I ask as I rub a hand down her bare back.

Later I'm going to give her that spanking...and so much more. But for now, I need time to recover, and I need to show her the town. Let her fall in love with the tiny mountain town of Crescent Ridge before she falls in love with me.

"Hell yes!" she shouts. "Are you freaking serious? Do they have a haunted house?"

She begins rambling, not waiting for me to answer any of her questions, excitement pouring off her in waves.

"It's my favorite holiday. I always try to hit as many haunted houses and trails as I can every year. My friends are *sick* of going with me."

"I don't know if they have a haunted house," I tell her, thinking about how the festival is more about face painting and pumpkin carving.

I see the disappointment dim her smile and I rush to add, "But there is a creepy graveyard."

"Aren't all graveyards creepy?" she retorts with her smile returning in full bloom.

"No, some are downright fancy with their neat little rows and their manicured lawns."

"Tell me more," she whispers into my ear as her hand paints lazy circles on my chest.

Looking down and noticing the gleam in her eye I don't fight my smirk. Bending the arm not holding her close I put my hand behind my head and let her see my bicep flex. She doesn't make it obvious that she notices but I see her pupils dilate.

"It's old, some of the gravestones can't be read they're so faded. The entire thing is overgrown with creeping vines and wildflowers. Some of the locals say they can hear the spirits whispering late at night," I say letting my voice go lower until it sounds downright sinister.

"You're pulling my leg," she says frowning.

"Nope," I say before flicking her scrunched up nose with the tip of my finger. "I'll show you tonight and let you see for yourself."

My answer seems to reassure her, and I can't stop myself from adding, "And if you're a good girl I'll bend you over one of those tombstones and fuck you until your soul leaves your body."

In answer her hand trails down the planes of my stomach until she reaches my cock. My traitorous cock that is hard and ready for another round. Emma's pleased murmur is enough to have it twitching against my stomach before she wraps her hand around it giving it a firm stroke.

I'm ready to roll over and show her the consequences of teasing me when she pushes on my chest as she sits up. I watch with wide eyes as she slides down the bed until she lays between my spread thighs. Her pale cheeks flush as she looks first at my cock and then at my face before licking the head.

"Emma-" I start to say.

I don't know what I was going to say next. One minute I'm talking and the next my mouth is hanging open while she does her damned best to suck my soul out of my body through the tip of my cock.

My hands grab the sheets on either side of my hips as she goes back down for another drag, her throat swallowing as she looks at me with large green eyes dark with desire. I see the devilish spark enter her eyes and I decide then and there that I'm going to fuck that pretty little mouth.

Her eyes get wider when my hands abandon their grip on the sheets to wind their way into her blonde hair. I give a slight tug to gauge her reaction, and the warm hum of her approval is all the permission I need. With dark lusty eyes she watches me as I guide her head up and down on my cock.

Her pink lips stretch so perfectly around my girth, the tiny freckle on her bottom lip nearly invisible as I drag her down my length.

Her hair tangles around my fingers so tightly they become white as I set a brutal pace. The wet sound of her mouth sucking my hard flesh has the darkness within me coming to life with a roar.

I come in her mouth with no warning, her eyes widen in surprise as she struggles to swallow every drop of my seed.

Releasing my hold on her hair I slump down on the bed. All the muscles that clenched when I came begin to relax, the warm soothing rush making me feel like I've just finished an intense workout at the gym.

Emma doesn't immediately join me. I watch with half lidded eyes as she wipes a bit of drool from her chin and then with a deviant glint in her green irises she latches onto my cock. Oversensitive from my orgasm my hips arch off the bed when she drags her tongue over the head of my cock. Each lick is its own torture as she watches me from underneath her lashes as she cleans my cock. Just when I don't think I can take anymore she releases me with an audible pop.

"Good boy," she purrs with a pleased smirk.

Can't have that.

"Come here," I say holding my arms out for her to come cuddle me.

She crawls up the bed until her head can rest solidly on my chest, but I don't give her the chance to relax. Grabbing her arm, I use her momentum to have her sprawl helplessly across my lap as I sit up.

"Thanks for the reminder, Babe," I say with a smile. "Being called a good boy reminded me what a *bad girl* you've been."

"Oh, no," she cries mockingly.

From this angle she can't see the smirk tugging at my lips. If she could, she might be a bit more serious. This isn't a funishment. It is a punishment, and by the end she's going to have a proper respect for me.

Ten solid strokes later and her tone is sincere once again.

"Who do you belong to?" I ask, using my grip on her hair to force her to look at me.

"You," she says her pools of emerald green watering with the aftermath of her spanking.

I help her sit up, her thighs landing on either side of mine. I wipe the tears away from her cheeks, wondering for a moment if I went too far. If I overplayed my hand and this is the moment where any hope for our future crashed and burned.

But then her smile returns, soft lips reddened from our earlier kisses stretching her mouth wide as she looks at me. Her hands land on my bare chest again and I shouldn't be surprised when she grinds herself against me. I noticed she was getting wet while I spanked her. The punishment for acting like a brat and trying to make me jealous made her ass red and I'm sure the pain will linger.

She coats my cock with her arousal as she grinds. God help me but her actions have me hardening underneath her. We need a break-to hydrate if nothing else. But as her movements continue, I find myself unable to stop her. Worse. I encourage it.

"Look at how needy you become in my bed," I say as I palm her breasts. "How desperately you need me to help you come."

I play with the soft flesh, kneading it gently as her breathing picks up. My tattoos seem bolder against her unmarked skin, the dark lines a stark contrast to the pale pink of her breasts.

As her head tips back, I take the opportunity to shift my hands from her breasts to her hips. Lifting her up I latch onto her nipple, tugging the sweet bud into my mouth.

Rolling it against my tongue I listen to her pleas and cries as I distract her from where I've lined myself up with her dripping pussy. Releasing her nipple, I let go of her hips and let her sit down on my lap once more. Her eyes open just in time to see me spear her with my cock.

"Good thing I love a needy cunt," I say before guiding her hips up and down, using her body to work my length.

Her gasp at my words turns into a moan as I set a slow pace, letting the heat build for both of us. With multiple orgasms neither of us is desperate to come. Not yet. This one will be slow and gentle.

"Andrew," she says my name softly like a prayer as she rides me. "I don't think I can."

"You didn't think that when you were teasing my cock with your dripping pussy," I say with a dark tone. "You'll come on my cock like a good girlfriend, won't you?"

The words spark something dark in her eyes. A possessive streak that matches my own. My girlfriend. *Mine.*

Unable to help myself as possession rolls through my veins, I drive my hips up to meet hers. Her moans turn to screams as I hold her above me, hammering into her pussy from below.

Her muscles clamp down on me as her orgasm drenches my cock. Those muscles squeezing my length and milking me for every drop of seed I have left as I come inside her pretty pink pussy with a roar.

Emma and I lay in a pile of limbs napping for a good chunk of the morning before I pull her into the shower in the late afternoon. If she's surprised that we shower together she doesn't comment. I wash and condition her hair, scratching her scalp softly with my nails as her eyes drift closed in contentment.

"We'll get lunch in town," I say while we dress.

While she rescheduled her flight for Sunday rather than tonight, I went out to the rental car and grabbed her luggage. Despite planning a shorter trip, her bag is stuffed with clothing, more than she would need for the weekend even. Emma hums her agreement for my lunch plan as she pulls on a black ruffled skirt that hits mid-thigh. It pairs well with her cream sweater.

"Your legs will get cold," I warn her. "When it gets dark the temperature drops rapidly in the mountains."

She holds up a pair of orange and black striped tights in response. I don't think it will be enough to keep the chill away, they stop above her knee. Not that I will complain about the eyeful of creamy skin it leaves on display.

I reach into the darkest recess of my closet to pull out a pair of black slacks and a dark grey sweater. It's the outfit I've used in the past for job interviews, and it is the nicest thing I have to wear. Watching as Emma curls her hair into loose waves, I feel the need to step up my game.

All the men at the festival will be wearing jeans and flannel shirts but I've always stood out. Slim and toned where the mountain men are broad and buff with muscles born of working outside in all elements. It's always been a tad off putting constantly comparing myself to them.

I catch her green-eyed gaze in the bathroom mirror when I come in to brush my teeth. I almost miss the way her eyes skim down the length of my body her pale cheeks flushing before her eyes dart back up to meet mine in the reflection. Emma's warm look of appreciation soothes the jagged edges of my pride. She barely spared Dave a glance at the diner. As farfetched as I find the possibility, it might just be possible that she would prefer me to the beefcakes wandering around.

A long drive up the mountain and I finally have Emma in Crescent Ridge. I see the way her eyes light up when she sees Main Street with its twin lines of shops. When it snows it looks like something straight out of a Hallmark movie and suddenly, I feel a dull ache in my chest when I think of Emma seeing that first snow in person.

"None of the businesses in my neighborhood bother decorating for Halloween," Emma tells me as we pass streetlights wrapped in orange and purple lights. Several full-size skeletons are posed on the sidewalk, some sitting on benches and others in more comical positions.

Emma laughs when we pass one that has its hand stuffed into an animatronic werewolf's mouth. With the festival in full swing, Main is packed with trucks, and we end up parking by Mrs. Carmichael's bakery, *Sugar Crossing*.

The plan was to pick up some sandwiches at the sub shop, but I can't deny Emma once she sees the window display. Cupcakes decorated with skulls, spiders, and broomsticks sit beside chocolate chip cookies shaped like pumpkins and witch hats.

Streamers of skeletons holding hands hang from the window and once we step inside, I notice the ceiling is covered in a fake spider web. Several plastic spiders hang suspended just above my head and Emma giggles when I run face first into one that I didn't see hanging lower.

"Andrew!" Mrs. Carmichael greets from behind her clear glass display counter. "It's been an age, if it's been a day! And who is this lovely woman? Finally send off for a bride of your own?"

I barely manage to fight my way out of the tangle of spider web while Emma introduces herself to the baker.

"Emma, pleased to meet you. I'm Andrew's girlfriend and I'm not a mail order bride. I love your shop!" she says in her bubbly manner.

"This is Mrs. Carmichael," I say stepping forward to finish introductions. "She's a local legend and can bake better than anyone you've seen on TV."

"Oh stop!" Mrs. Carmichael says waving a wrinkled hand to fight off my praise. "I just love baking and the boys love sweets."

The boys she refers to are fully grown lumberjacks who stand larger than the trees they cut down. Three sons who tower over their mother and can eat their way through a couple dozen cupcakes each. Emma already met Tobias, the eldest son at the diner.

Small with a grey bun, Mrs. Carmichael bustles around packing and ringing up our order. A chocolate chip witch hat for me and a skull cupcake for Emma. I wave her away when she offers to pay. She's spending the weekend in my town when she didn't plan to, and I'll be damned if the impulsive decision costs her a single dime.

"Face painting!" Emma shouts when she sees the advertisement in the window of the barbershop. "We *have* to get our faces painted."

I follow along as she leads me through the town. By the time we reach the hayride that will take us down to the festival proper she's met everyone. Thanks to the barbershop my face looks like a skull, fitting with my dark color scheme, and Emma has spider webs in purple and black that start at the crown of her head and arch down to her cheeks.

We've eaten our sweet treats and downed matching cups of warm apple cider, the sugar hitting Emma's bloodstream and causing her to vibrate on the haybale beside me.

Her hand wrapped in mine, the roses and thorns sheltering her soft skin from the chilly evening air. Throughout our exploration of the town, she held my hand constantly and the few times we separated she stayed close never more than an arm length away.

In less than a day I've become accustomed to her casual touches. More than accustomed. Addicted.

The way she skips from booth to booth at the festival lights my heart. I'm dragged in her wake as she tugs me along, her excitement overflowing as her curls bounce along her back. She barely refrains from squealing when she spots the coffee tent.

Bean There is a lovely shop that I don't frequent often. In truth I prefer to keep to myself. I've interacted with more people today than in the last month, thanks in no small part to Emma. She does bring out the best in me.

Mama Mary flags us down after we have matching pumpkin spiced lattes in hand. A petite woman with short silver hair she's Daniel Hart's mother but for those of us without family on the ridge she's become a surrogate mother.

"Is this the Emma, I've heard so much about?" she asks before immediately pulling my girlfriend into a hug without waiting for an answer.

"Yes," I reply, "Emma this is Mama Mary. She's a bit of a mother to most of us, hence the nickname."

Emma watches fondly as Mary grabs me in a tight hold. She pinches my cheek before letting us continue on our way with a promise to visit her soon.

Emma

I'm drunk on sugar, caffeine, and Andrew's intoxicating presence as I lead him through the festival grounds. A half dozen times I consider apologizing but each time I stop and begin to regulate my excitement I see his smile and bite back my words. Unlike so many others his patience doesn't wear thin under my unwavering barrage of enthusiasm.

"There is a maze," Andrew says leaning down to speak into my ear unbothered by the loud crowd of people mingling around us as we sip our lattes.

"Haunted?" I ask a bit breathlessly.

"Yes, but will a corn maze be enough?" he whispers back.

Judging by the dark look in his blue eyes he can read the thrum of desire burning in my veins. The thrill of the scare and the impending chase. The fear of not being able to find the exit as panic whips into a frenzy.

"Perfect," I say with a bright smile no doubt a bit heavy on the teeth.

Without another word he directs me through the pedestrian traffic, finding a trash can for our cups on the way as he cuts a path through the stream of people. Every man we pass is draped in flannel and looks to be cut from the mountain we're standing on.

The girls back home would be too busy drooling over the mass of muscles walking around to notice the scent of roasted corn mingling with the cinnamon and nutmeg wafting over from the coffee tent. They would completely miss the slender man with tattoos, dark hair, and freckles I can't stop touching.

It's a miracle he hasn't complained about how I'm clinging to him like a barnacle on a ship's hull.

We wait in a long line for our turn in the maze every few minutes shuffling forward a few steps as people chatter around us. Several children run amok, most in their Halloween costumes. A bumblebee chases a witch with a bright green face. A ninja throws a corndog at a princess calling her snooty. Their laughter is high pitched carrying over the other sounds and I find myself entranced watching them run about.

"Do you want children?" Andrew's deep baritone takes me by surprise.

His chest is warm against my back, his arms wrapped loosely around my waist as he rests his chin on top of my head.

"Eventually," I answer. "You?"

"Impartial," he says just loud enough for me to hear. "But willing."

"I've always wanted three," I reply. "I have an older brother, but I always wanted a sister."

"Only child, but I would have liked having a sibling or two to share my childhood," he replies as we step forward. "I have divorced parents, who like to pretend the other doesn't exist. My presence makes that exceedingly difficult, so we speak twice a year and occasionally meet up for dinner when the guilt gets to them."

"I'm sorry," I whisper, squeezing his wrist with a gentle pressure that I hope is soothing.

"Don't be," he answers. "They were worse together. I will take apathy over fury any day. And their mistakes helped me learn what makes a relationship work. What makes it last through the trials and tribulations of life."

"Care to share your grand epiphany?" I ask.

"Three things closely entwined," he whispers into my ear, his warm breath sending chills down my arms.

"Passion," he says as he places a chaste kiss on my neck.

I should be shying away from his public display, but I can't bring myself to. Other couples are kissing and cuddling around us. Our little display is pure by comparison.

It's the entirely impure memory of this morning that has me rubbing my thighs together discreetly.

"Obsession." His tattooed hand leaves my waist and wraps loosely around my throat.

The way his thumb strokes the long column of my neck has me trembling in Andrew's embrace. The way we cling to one another in bed and the way we click together like two long lost puzzle pieces always meant to join. It steals my breath from my lungs.

"Love." His voice is barely audible.

My heart stops dead in my chest at the word. A word so heavy and bold I can't breathe. I know he's not declaring his love for me. It's too soon. Logic wars with emotion as I inexplicably long for it to be more than a word.

I want his passion and obsession. I want his love.

No matter how short the timeframe it doesn't stop the pang of longing that fills my chest with my next breath.

"Loyalty," I say adding a fourth as I squeeze the hand still wrapped around my waist as I lean back into his hold.

His murmur of agreement stirs the fine hairs around my ear. We move forward with the line in silence, the weight of our words hanging heavy in the air.

When it's our turn the scarecrow running the maze hands us glow sticks. The faint screams of other entrants hit our ears, and I can't stop myself from grinning. Andrew follows behind me as I lead us into the maze.

The corn is a head taller than Andrew, the stalks planted so closely together that they form a wall on either side of us as we follow the path. A breeze blows through allowing the stalks to wave slightly in the wind, the leaves rustling as they brush against each other.

As the breeze stops, the rustling doesn't. My ears strain for any hint of sound as we come across the first split in the path marked by a jack o' lantern. Andrew's fingers trail down the back of my arm and I toss a grin over my shoulder at him.

Just as I'm about to ask left or right I see a large shadow move behind Andrew.

"Run!" I shout.

The grim reaper who bursts out of the wall of corn swipes at us with their scythe as we dart away laughing. Our feet slam into the soil the sound loud even to my own ears. We pause at the next intersection, our breathing coming out in heavy gasps.

Without hesitation Andrew reaches out and takes my hand pulling me down the path on the right. I fall into step beside him. A far off scream causes me to flinch drawing a laugh from Andrew.

His blue eyes are bright glowing in the dim light from the full moon as he steers us along the path. I've never felt safer and simultaneously more on edge in my life.

Twice more we turn right and finally we reach a dead end. Doubling back the rumbling sound of a chainsaw sends my stomach churning as we run away without looking back.

"Is it just me or is this maze bigger on the inside?" I joke.

Glancing at my watch I see we've been in the maze for almost twenty minutes, and I can't hear the festival anymore. I know we're still on the correct path. It's lined with solar lights to keep us from tripping in the dark.

"Did you see the exit when we were in line?" Andrew asks.

I think back and although we saw dozens of people enter, I can't remember seeing any leave.

"No," I say quietly.

We walk in silence, hands still clasped between us as we wordlessly make our way back to the jack o' lantern. On this side of the path, I notice an orange sign staked in the ground with black lettering.

Feel like you've been here before?

I point out the sign to Andrew and we share a laugh. Taking the other path Andrew leads us down another fork choosing to go left. As I'm about to ask if he can hear anything a clown mask pops out of the corn beside me, and I scream.

Andrew pulls me away as my scream turns into a giggle.

"Fucking clowns," he mutters when we're far enough away the scare actor can't hear us.

"Not a fan?" I ask in a teasing tone.

I'm already wondering if I can get him to wear some face paint and chase me through the woods. Less birthday party or rodeo clown and more dark jester.

"Not a chance," Andrew says without looking at me. "Don't even think about it."

"Too late," I reply smiling cheekily.

His huff of laughter reaches my ears as we follow a curve in the path. The next fork has an altar set up with battery operated candles with plastic flames and jars of herbs sitting on a blood-stained tattered cloth. A sign sits in the middle of the table with two hands pointing in different directions.

Left or Right?
Live or Die?

"Do we go left?" I ask. "And choose life? Or is the sign just there to throw us off?"

"We might not even be close to the end," Andrew replies.

"Let's go," I say choosing the right path.

Andrew follows gamely as we amble forward. We reach another dead end with dozens of plastic tombstones and signs decrying our impending doom. We turn to retrace our steps, and a little girl steps out of the corn wearing a blue dress with ruffles and her blonde hair in pigtails. She squeezes a brown teddy bear to her chest as she twirls in front of us.

"You shouldn't be here," she says in a sing song voice. "The ghosts don't like the living."

She comes to a stop in front of us allowing us to see the heavy shadows painted beneath her eyes and the grey color of her skin. As she talks, I notice the line of fake blood painted on her neck.

"Only the dead linger here," a voice says behind us.

Andrew and I turn simultaneously to see the looming figure of a skeleton standing behind us.

"Run!" the little girl yells before releasing a high-pitched giggle.

We run without stopping back to the altar and hit the other path at a jog. We turn a corner, and the bright lights of the festival cause me to squint as we exit the maze.

Andrew spots a photographer set up nearby and walks us over. Dried corn and maize hangs from a pergola and the laminated backdrop has *Crescent Ridge 18th Annual Fall Festival* printed in bold black letters over some cartoon pumpkins.

"Proof we survived the maze," Andrew whispers in my ear while the photographer directs us into a pose underneath the pergola. "And documentation of our first official date."

He stands behind me with his arms wrapped around my torso as we pose for the photo. The warm puff of his breath on my chilled skin has me fighting back a shiver as I smile for the camera.

Andrew

"I was promised a graveyard." Emma's tone is teasing as I lead her back to my truck.

"Don't worry, I always keep my promises," I tell her as I hold open her door and offer her a hand up into the cab.

Her eyebrow flies up to her hairline, her face skeptical.

"It's a short drive," I promise before shutting her door.

Emma keeps up a constant chatter as I drive. She talks about the locals and their overly nosy questions.

"I swear I was asked no less than five times if I was a mail order bride," she says as the truck climbs a particularly steep hill.

"Women don't move out here for the scenery," I reply. "It's a small town and we're not exactly a tourist destination."

I can share her disbelief over the constant supply of brides choosing to marry the men of Crescent Ridge. I didn't think mail order brides were even a thing anymore before I moved out here. But they are and most of the couples I've met found each other through a mail order bride program. Some describe it as a dating app but for marriage.

Last week I couldn't imagine marrying a woman without dating her first. Now as I watch Emma talk animatedly with her hands waving as she illustrates her points, I don't find the idea so outrageous. If Emma signed up for the program, I would bend over backwards to convince her to pick me as her husband. Maybe the mountain men of Crescent Ridge have the right idea.

I pull into the gravel parking lot just outside the cemetery gates. The cemetery itself is on a hill with hundreds of graves dotting the site. All the graves are centuries old, with anyone who has died in the last century buried in Bramble's cemetery at the base of the mountain. This is no longer a location of grieving but rather a historical site that genealogists visit from time to time.

Turning off the truck, we're in complete darkness as we exit. With only the light of the moon, we make our way to the gate. Although it's closed there isn't a lock or a groundskeeper to prevent us from entering.

"Going to throw me a bone, Andrew?" she teases as we walk up the winding path that leads into the cemetery.

"Does the idea of a bunch of ghosts watching me fuck you get you wet?" I whisper into her ear. The autumn air has a chill to it, but I know the goosebumps running down her arms are from my breath on her heated skin.

"Maybe it's just the thought of getting railed on a tombstone under a full moon."

"Liar," I say leaning close enough to have my lips brush the shell of her ear. "You like the idea of showing them how well this hot little pussy takes my cock. How wet you get every time I fuck you like a good little slut. You're gonna come on that stone and let it drip down so they get a taste of what it's like to feel alive."

I don't comment on the audible hitch in her breath my words trigger. Guiding her off the stone path we walk across the grass passing statues of angels and busts made to resemble the dearly departed.

"Where do you want me?" she asks surveying the assortment of graves surrounding us.

I don't know if it's the late hour or the location that's got chills running down my spine, but my cock is hard as Emma prances in front of me. Her skirt lifts briefly as a breeze blows through blessing me with a glimpse of her bare ass. The wink she shoots over her shoulder tells me everything I need to know.

I don't deign to respond to her question. I grab her wrist tugging her over to a sunken mausoleum. Leading her down the stone steps I swing open the heavy door brushing aside the cobwebs hanging down as I drag her to the center of the crypt.

Caskets line the walls with brass plates listing the names and birth and death dates. Emma gasps as she looks around the room, but she doesn't look frightened. Her eyes shine with an eagerness I should have expected.

"Here?" Emma asks with the slightest tremble in her voice.

If I didn't know her, I would attribute it to fear rather than excitement. Pressing close I slip a hand underneath her skirt, my fingers finding her bare pussy with ease.

"You're fucking soaked, Emma," I growl as I lean her back on the stone slab sitting in the middle of the room.

"Fuck me, Andrew," she pleads as her knees fall open putting her wet pussy on display.

The pale pink lips are shiny with arousal even with the little light making its way to us. Just the sight of her spread out like a feast ready for the taking is twisting my stomach into knots. Despite her urgency I don't give in to her demands. She's not the one in control and she needs a reminder.

I slap her clit with a light tap of my fingers. Her resulting yelp brings a smirk to my face.

"You're in no position to give orders," I say as I stroke a finger over her clit.

Seeing her shiver underneath my touch elicits a possessive urge to pin her down and pound my cock into her until she comes screaming my name.

"Please," she pleads as I rub stiff fingers through her wet folds.

She tries to wiggle her hips in a bid to get closer, to fuck herself on my fingers, but I put a quick stop to that. With a firm hand I press her hips down hindering her movements and causing her to groan.

"Listen to you," I say as I thrust my fingers into her sharply pulling yet another moan from her lips. "Moaning and groaning like a ghost. If anyone wanders by this graveyard tonight, they'll think this place is truly haunted."

With her head tossed back as she strains against my restricting hand in vain, I doubt she's following the flow of my words. Seeing her eyes squeezed shut tempts me to slap her clit again, but I don't want to pull my fingers out of her pussy.

"Emma," I purr as I lean over her.

My fingers go still just shy of her G-spot.

"A-Andrew," she moans in supplication.

"Emma," I say. "Let me see those pretty green eyes."

Her lashes part and I get the tiniest glimpse of emerald before I curl my fingers brushing her G-spot and she closes her eyes again.

"Emma," I murmur in admonishment.

This time her eyes open wider, the brilliant green flashing with annoyance that I've stopped my exploration again.

"Andrew," she chides. "If you don't-"

My fingers slip out before she finishes saying my name. The second slap to her clit cuts off her sentence abruptly.

"You're not in charge, Babe," I tell her letting my smugness color my tone.

She lies beneath me compliant as I return my fingers to her pussy. Her eyes fixate on me, the pupils blown wide nearly swallowing the green rings as I pump my fingers. I can't look away from her eyes as she begins to breathe in heavy gasps that match the pace of my fingers.

Wet squelching sounds echo around the stones surrounding us as Emma's muscles begin to flutter and pulse around my fingers. The obscene sounds go straight to my cock making my blood rush south as it goes impossibly harder. I can feel the zipper carving a pattern into the hard flesh.

"Soak this stone," I command as she clamps down. "Give these ghosts a taste of your juicy pussy."

Her body goes tight like it's seizing her arms and legs flexing as she comes around my fingers. The muscles squeezing me milk my fingers in a shallow imitation of what will happen when she comes again on my cock.

Inaudible grumbling meets my ears when I withdraw my fingers. Sucking the pair into my mouth I close my eyes when the taste of Emma bursts on my tongue.

"Eyes on me, Babe," Emma says nudging my hip with her bent knee.

She lies before me, body slack and satisfied but there is a dark hunger in her eyes begging for more. Begging for every inch of my cock and every drop of pleasure I can wring from her body.

I let her teasing command slide, ignoring her mocking tone as I unbuckle my belt, tapping the metal frame against the inside of her thigh. She shies away from the cold touch of steel as I finish freeing my cock from the harsh confines of my pants. Rising onto her elbows she eyes me with a blatant hunger that causes my chest to swell with male pride.

None of those mountain men could handle this woman. They might have stacks of muscles but not a single damn one of them would match her level of kink. None of them would bring her to orgasm in a graveyard surrounded by skeletons and restless spirits.

A chill wind blows through the open door carrying the short howls of a pack of coyotes. Emma freezes underneath me, her expression morphing from arousal to fear as she reaches out to grasp my forearms. Her nails bite into my skin as I smile down at my girlfriend.

"Not afraid of ghosts haunting us for desecrating their sacred resting place but a pack of coyotes has you running scared?" I ask as I rub the head of my cock through her slick lips.

"One is a far more pressing danger," she scolds even as I see the spark of desire reignite in her green eyes.

A single thrust has me sliding into the hilt the low timber of my moan overshadowing her breathy gasp.

"The door is open," Emma protests even as she clutches me closer as I begin to move my hips. "They can come in."

I let her panic build for a moment, the fear adding to her arousal as I thrum her clit with my thumb in time with my thrusts.

"They're not close by," I reassure her.

My hands push her thighs to the side splaying her open to allow my cock to sink deeper.

"You can't know that," she argues.

Emma is close to the edge again, her breath coming in short fast puffs that are visible in the chilly air.

"Too weak," I mutter between thrusts, doing my best to stave off my own orgasm. "They're miles away."

Her eyes are wide open watching the door over my shoulder and the irritation that she doesn't trust me to protect her at her most vulnerable causes me to pinch her clit in reproach.

"I'm the only creature you need to be worried about right now," I say when her eyes dart back to my face.

Without missing a beat, I reach out and wrap my hand around her throat. The black ink of my tattoos looks beautiful against her flushed skin. Squeezing gently, I see the exact moment she forgets about the coyotes. They're still howling, the sounds slowly growing quieter as they move further away.

"A pretty girl like you doesn't need to worry about anything other than gripping my cock tight and coming like you're told," I say.

Unable to argue with my hand around her throat she melts under the force of my thrusts as I drive her closer to the edge. I don't let up with her compliance. Emma's fingers turn white as they grip my forearms, her eyes liquid pools of desire as she comes on my cock.

I continue thrusting through her orgasm until I can't ignore the tight grip of her warmth anymore and I come with a loud moan. Emma's hands comb through my hair as I lay slumped against her chest. The steady rise and fall of her chest with every breath soothing me as she strokes her hands down my neck and begins kneading my shoulders.

A breeze causes us both to shiver and I pull back with reluctance. Maybe we'll repeat this little act on a warm summer night but right now I need to get Emma into the truck so she can warm up before she catches a cold. Pulling off my sweater I stuff it over her head without acknowledging her protests.

"You'll get cold," she murmurs even as she sticks her arms through the sleeves.

She swims in folds of fabric, the hem falling lower than her skirt as she stands up on wobbly legs. Her curls are destroyed, leaving her with a frizzy blonde halo and I can't hide my dopey smile.

"What?" she asks when she notices me staring. "Do I have coffee breath?"

She begins to ramble. Of course, we both have coffee breath, but I don't see how that could be an issue. I like the taste of pumpkin spice on her tongue. Leaning over I kiss her until she melts against me, all worries and concerns gone with the wind.

Her fingers go to my belt buckle, and I swat her away with a laugh.

"Home," I scold her as I grab her hand and begin leading her back to the truck. "It's getting too cold for another round. The ghosts will just have to be satisfied with the show they got."

Emma

One long weekend with the man of my dreams and reality comes crashing down Sunday morning. I'm expected back at work on Monday and that means I have a flight to catch. No more mind-blowing sex or cuddles in my immediate future.

"I wish I didn't have to leave," I tell him. "My job and my friends would lose their minds if I didn't go back home though. I didn't tell them I was meeting anyone this weekend."

His blue eyes flick to mine angrily from where he is unloading the dishwasher. Aside from another trip to the diner and the festival foods we scarfed down, Andrew has made all our meals, and for a man living alone on a mountain he is a fantastic cook.

"Are you serious?" he snaps.

For a moment I think he's outraged that I kept him a secret.

"You came to meet a random man without telling anyone? What if I were a serial killer?" he adds before I can reply.

His hands are in his hair and he's pacing the length of his kitchen barefoot while I stand in the doorway watching him.

"You're not," I mumble.

"You didn't know that three days ago!" he shouts, raising his hands above his head as if to direct an airplane onto a runway.

"Congrats!" I say sarcastically. "Now you sound like a psycho."

"Good!" he says matching my tone. "I need to be one to look after you."

"I don't need you to look after me," I snarl.

As if I need a fucking keeper. I'm a full-grown woman and I don't need a man to take care of me. I got enough of that treatment from my parents and my brother. I don't need it from Andrew too.

"Your pussy says otherwise," he replies with a smug look as if the argument is settled.

His words shock me into silence long enough for him to grab a duffel bag out of his closet. I watch as he begins folding shirts and jeans before stuffing them in the bag.

"Where are you going?" I ask a little miffed that he's that eager to get away from me that he can't wait for me to leave for the airport.

"Atlanta, apparently," he mutters as he adds socks and underwear to the bag.

"Seriously?" I ask even as I grab his cell phone charger and laptop from beside the bed and hand them to him.

"Yes. I'm not letting a sexual deviant like you roam freely in a city full of innocent unsuspecting people." His tone is serious but the slight smirk curling his lips says otherwise.

"I didn't invite you," I say crossing my arms and trying to act nonchalant when inside I'm a puddle of goo.

This isn't the end. We're not parting ways to inevitably end up in a frustrating long-distance relationship held together by willpower and video chats.

"Your mouth didn't but something else sure did," he says before his eyes drop to where the zipper of my jeans hides me from his gaze.

"Stop that!" I scold.

His answering laugh makes my heart skip a beat as I try not to blush. The deep rumbly baritone never fails to send my heart racing. Not to mention its effect on *other* areas of my body.

"Hurry up or we're going to miss our flight," Andrew says as he walks by to get something from his closet.

His hand smacks my ass on the way and despite the thick fabric of my skirt my ass is still stinging when he returns with a pair of over the ear headphones clasped in his hands. The smirk is a permanent fixture at this point and while I'd love to wipe it from his face a quick glance at the clock proves his point.

We don't have time to waste.

"You don't have a ticket," I mutter wondering if I can reschedule my flight again.

Surely the travel insurance will cover a last-minute cancellation. Instead of flying out this morning we can leave tonight. And it will give Andrew more time to pack to ensure he doesn't forget anything.

"Bought one yesterday," Andrew says as he hands me his phone to show me his ticket information.

For all the sudden argument and packing this isn't a last-minute decision on his part. He wanted it to be a surprise. His stuffed duffel bag lands next to my sticker slapped suitcase and he looks at me expectantly.

Waiting for me to agree. To invite him. I know without a doubt if I said no, he wouldn't follow me. Andrew is without a doubt a good man and a gentleman. Both rare qualities on their own never mind the statistics of finding both in a single man.

"Let's go," I say trying for a tone of exasperation but judging by the broad smile on Andrew's face my excitement is obvious.

I can't hide my feelings from this man. He sees right through my layers to the darkest hidden corners of my soul with ease. As he grabs our luggage before walking me out to my rental car, I can admit at least to myself that I don't want to hide them anymore. Not from Andrew.

There's something building between us. Something I'm scared to name but desperate to explore, and I think Andrew feels it too.

Andrew

Catching our flight out of Bramble is easy. The airport is tiny with only a few flights leaving each day. A few years ago, we would have had to fly out in a puddle jumper rather than a 747. Ignoring the call for first class boarding I sit with Emma until her group is called. She was quiet the entire ride over and I can see the nervous pulse fluttering in her neck every few minutes.

She's nervous. Maybe about the flight but more likely she's having second thoughts about our relationship and how quickly it's progressing. I'm no fool. I know that I'm speeding things along at a reckless pace, but I can't help it. If I don't give this everything I have, then I know I'll regret it for the rest of my life.

A woman like Emma is a once in a lifetime kind of find. Everything about us clicks together so seamlessly, so perfectly. Even the odd parts.

"Nice," Emma says as I plop down into the seat beside her.

The man who I exchanged seats with ambles away with the first class ticket I purchased clutched between his fingers with a gleeful expression. I didn't want to rely on a random stranger's kindness, so I bought a better seat hoping to entice Emma's seatmate with an upgrade and it worked.

"I wasn't going to let my girlfriend sit by herself," I say nonchalantly.

Emma's hand grabs mine with an unexpected fierceness. Her nails cut into the soft flesh of my palm like tent stakes driving into dirt.

"I can't decide if that makes you chivalrous or possessive," she whispers mindful of the people seated around us.

"Both," I whisper back.

Her delighted giggle is enough to have me grinning like a lovesick dope during takeoff. She clings to me the entire time wrapped around my arm like she's afraid I'll vanish if she lets go.

Once we're in the air and all the other passengers are preoccupied with their books or the in-flight movie I lean over to whisper in Emma's ear.

"I have a fantasy I'd like you to consider."

She doesn't respond verbally but I see the way she bites her bottom lip to keep from smiling and the way her green eyes glint with desire.

"Ever fancy joining the mile high club?" I ask letting my lips graze her ear as I whisper the words.

"I'm game," she whispers back and after some furtive glances to ensure the coast is clear I lead the way to the bathroom.

Ridiculously tiny, there is barely enough room for us both to stand with the door closed. I nearly suggest ditching the entire idea but then Emma brushes against me and all the blood rushes from my brain to my cock.

"You are going to need to be quiet," I whisper as Emma sits on the sink.

"You're the one with the filthy mouth," she retorts.

"I was referring to the way you moan every time I fuck you," I say as I unbuckle my belt.

"I do not-" she begins to argue, her voice rising without her notice, and I lunge forward to silence her.

Our kiss isn't sweet or gentle. Emma matches my aggression with equal fervor, her teeth biting at my bottom lip and her tongue darting forward to tangle with mine. She doesn't let me move an inch as she attacks my mouth barely giving me enough space to free my cock and flip up her skirt.

I thrust, her pussy slick and hot as she takes every inch. I swallow her moans even as I grab her hips and hold her in place as I begin fucking her. We don't have time to linger if we don't want to get caught.

She clutches my shoulders through my shirt, the nails biting into my skin despite the thin cotton barrier. I'm helpless to do anything more than drive my hips into hers seeking relief for the heat climbing up my spine as she clings to me.

When our mouths part and I suck in a deep breath of air, Emma lets out a moan. I slap a hand over her mouth, but I worry the damage is done. The sounds of our bodies meeting are loud enough in the tiny room. Emma's green eyes flare bright as she continues to moan against my palm. With my hand clasped tightly over her mouth she's free to make as many sounds as she wants.

I'm the one who has to keep their mouth shut to avoid discovery and it's harder than I expected not to tell Emma exactly what she's doing to me. How her body bends eagerly to my will and how much I like the way she moans every time she takes my cock.

Her teeth bite down on the flesh of my palm when she comes, her scream muffled. Her muscles clamping down on my cock drags my orgasm from the steady build of warmth to a blazing inferno of heat in seconds. Helpless to prolong our pleasure, I come in Emma with a loud moan closing my eyes and throwing my head back.

When I open my eyes, Emma is looking at me with a mixture of contentment and trepidation.

Shit.

Righting our clothes takes a moment and some careful maneuvering. No matter how I try to smooth down my hair it springs back up in willful clumps. Emma is no better, her cheeks are still flushed and there is a clear red imprint from where my hand was over her mouth. Only an idiot wouldn't know what we've been up to. At least the marks on Emma's face will fade in a few minutes.

A loud knock on the door makes us both freeze, looking at each other with wide eyes.

"It's going to be a while," I call out. "Flying never agrees with me!"

Emma's hands fly up to cover her mouth as she struggles to muffle her giggles. The masculine sigh on the other side of the door precedes a grumble before we hear the man walk away. Our eyes meet knowingly. If we can hear his footsteps there is no telling what anyone walking by could hear.

"I'll go first," I tell Emma. "Wait five minutes and follow."

I want to gauge the situation and do what I can to mitigate any embarrassment before she leaves the bathroom.

Pressing one last chaste kiss to her lips I slip out the door. Walking back to our seats nothing seems out of place. Everyone is still dialed into their choice of distraction. Just as I reach our seats, I hear Emma's soft footsteps behind me. I don't address her disobedience with words. My eyebrow rises in reproach, but Emma doesn't look remorseful. She knows just as well as I do how it looks for us both to walk back together. I meet the eye of an elderly woman, looking over at us from across the aisle. Her cloudy brown eyes are hidden behind thick tortoise shell glasses, but her smile is knowing. She winks at me before turning back to her ereader.

"We need to work on your discretion," I murmur to Emma as I open the little bottle of water the attendant provided after takeoff.

She peers at me from beneath her lashes as she scans me with a keen eye.

"I'm not the one who couldn't help but moan like a whore when he came." Her soft-spoken words cause me to choke on my water.

"You're going to pay for that dirty mouth," I growl into her ear.

Relaxing back into my seat, I settle in to watch the comedy playing on the small screen attached to the back of the seat in front of me. Emma's head lands softly on my shoulder as she cuddles close to me, her eyes fixed on the same screen.

By the time the credits roll the attendants are directing us to fasten our seatbelts for landing. Emma's hands clutch my arm tightly while we taxi down the runway.

"I can't wait to get home," Emma says to me as we walk through the metropolitan airport in search of the baggage claim.

"Exhausted from roughing it in the mountains?" I tease knocking my shoulder against hers.

"Hardly roughing it," she replies with a giggle. "Your cabin is huge compared to my apartment. Just you wait and see."

As Emma watches for our luggage, I clear my throat. No time like the present to bring up something a little awkward.

"I was thinking I could stay in a hotel while I'm here," I say fixing my eyes on the spinning carousel loaded with bags. "I don't want to cramp your style."

"Don't be stupid," Emma says shortly. "Cramp my style? That phrase is older than my grandpa. You need to get out more."

Her words are reassuring but I can't help but feel that I'm pushing her into a situation that she might find uncomfortable.

"You weren't expecting to come home with a guest much less a boyfriend in tow and-" I begin to rationalize but she cuts me off.

"I stayed in your home. You'll stay in mine." She glares, daring me with her eyes to disagree with her again and I swallow the rest of my protest.

"Now be a darling and grab our bags," she says rocking back on her heels. "I'm still a little *exhausted* from the plane ride. I've got this tight spot in my lower back from sitting awkwardly."

I bite my bottom lip to stop myself from grinning as I lean over to grab her suitcase and my duffel.

"I'll rub it later," I tell her as she leads us out of the airport.

The crowd of bodies surrounding us is overwhelming at first, but Emma doesn't seem bothered. I keep my eyes on her as she floats ahead of me making a direct line for a parking garage.

I nearly die when she leads me to her car. In a lot filled with sedans, vans, and trucks in neutral colors she has the only car wrapped in a bright red color with a character from *Legion X* sprawled across the hood.

"You nerd," I say between laughs.

"Shut it," she replies with a fierce scowl.

Riding in the passenger seat of her car is an experience. During the quick drive to her apartment, I had no shortage of fidgets and baubles to play with, which was a good thing considering how nerve wracking the trip was. The mini Rubik's cube I found in the center console saved my sanity. I was right to worry about Emma driving down the mountain. The woman could barely manage to drive from the airport to her apartment complex without getting into an accident.

No turn signals. Zero attention to blind spots. And an inhumane rage directed at her fellow drivers for simply existing. It would be a civil service to disconnect and hide her battery. The Atlanta PD might just give me a medal.

The complex is brick with a glass front door that doesn't lock, and the entire lobby smells like mildew. I ignore the urge to wrinkle my nose, but the disgust must show on my face because she immediately adopts a sheepish expression.

"Cosplay is an expensive hobby, and this was the cheapest option that made sense," she says as she leads me over to a flight of stairs. "The neighborhood is decent and it's close to my work and downtown."

I don't comment on the elevator that has a faded out of order sign taped to it. Or the carpeted steps that are an unsettling shade of brown. Everywhere I look as we climb thirteen flights of steps is another reason not to live here. I hate cities. I went to college in Chicago and four years later I couldn't get far enough away from the crowds.

Emma's apartment number is 13b and her door is made of the same cheap particle board as the rest of her floor. She grumbles as she fights with the lock for a few moments, the latch sticking before she manages to shoulder it open. I could open her front door with a butter knife easier than with her key. The door creaks open and I make a note to pick up some WD-40 for the latch and the hinges. And a few other things to make her home more secure.

"Don't get the wrong idea," she tells me as she leads me into her apartment. "It's only this tidy because I wanted to come back to a clean home."

Her home is a reflection of her, bright and warm with a distinct lavender scent that instantly makes me feel at home despite the unfamiliar surroundings. It's a two bedroom apartment, and her bedroom has a bed large enough for us to share with a black and white sheet set with a spiderweb pattern embroidered on the comforter buried underneath a dozen pillows in matching colors.

The entire apartment screams her love for the spooky holiday. Fake spiderwebs and tattered cloth drapes every available surface, and she has bloody decals scattered around her walls. Fake skulls decorate her coffee table, and she has several white pillar candles littered throughout the apartment.

The other bedroom is sparse with no other furniture than a desk buried under mounds of aluminum.

"Some are for me, and some are custom orders from people I meet at conventions," she tells me when I ask about the chain mail armor replicas.

"Nice little side hustle, I compliment.

"More like obsession," she says as she walks over to the closet door to reveal dozens of completed sets.

"Is that one from *Medieval Slayer*?" I ask pointing at a bright red set.

"Yes!" She answers with pride, "You play?"

We talk video games as she unpacks her suitcase and makes room for my clothes in her closet. She doesn't ask how long I'm staying and I'm grateful for that small mercy, because I don't have an answer.

A week. Maybe more if we continue to click like we have this past weekend. I can work from anywhere, and working from Emma's home with its navy blue walls and overabundance of soft pillows wouldn't be a chore.

Everywhere I look there is evidence of Emma. Mugs with nerdy quotes in the kitchen and framed movie posters hanging on the living room walls. I hate the city but I'm beginning to think I could love her enough to live anywhere.

Emma

"What do you want for dinner?" I ask from the pile of blankets I am currently bundled inside.

"I think a black hole swallowed the contents of your fridge," he replies from his seat on the couch sans blanket.

Too hot he complains, but he still lets me snuggle against his side.

"Obviously I meant takeout," I say poking a finger into his side. "Chinese, Mexican, or pizza?"

"Hm," he hums noncommittedly as he considers the options.

I have dozens of menus pinned to the fridge. He doesn't know it yet but he's not only going to fetch one but also place the order. I'll pay for it, but I am done peopling today. First the close confines of the plane and then the crowded airport were too much.

Andrew begins peeling back my blankets despite my grumbled protests. Once he has wiggled his way into my cocoon, he curls his long body around mine, the heat of his body too much in addition to the multiple layers.

"I *am* hungry," he whispers, blowing warm air against my neck. "But not for food."

"Insatiable," I whisper back before his lips claim mine.

Compared to our rushed encounter on the plane this time we linger in every moment and every kiss. He kisses me like the world stands still around us. The wet hot press of his lips to mine has the tips of my fingers tingling with static. My hot core beats in time with my heart, the blood a dull roar in my ears with each pulse. Uncaring if I appear needy, I claw at his clothes like a woman possessed.

He doesn't laugh or tease me as I strip him of his clothes. A fond indulgent smile curves the corners of his lips up as he watches me with those bright blue eyes behind his glasses.

Minutes or hours pass as I explore the vast expanse of his chest and stomach. The faint line of dark hair that leads beneath the heavy denim waistband of his jeans finally drawing my attention. A noticeable bulge strains against the zipper but I'm in no rush. Not yet.

"You look a little warm," Andrew murmurs before I drag my nails lightly down his chest.

His resounding moan causes another pulse between my thighs. I could strip him of his pants and ride him to completion right now. My orgasm would come fast and easy, but I want to stretch this out.

Savor this man and his delectable body. Sear the image of him arching into my touch into my very brain. I want to live in this moment forever.

Andrew helps me peel out of my clothes, the chilly apartment air doing nothing to dampen the heat building between us. The way our bodies slide against each other is a dance unlike any other.

"Open up for me," he says as he tilts me back on the couch, the pile of blankets underneath my back.

My thighs fall open leaving my pussy exposed as he rocks back onto his heels to stare at me.

"So pretty," he whispers more to himself than to me.

His fingers part my folds, and I watch as he looks at my dripping center. His blue eyes darken with a fierce hunger as they fixate on my clit. The pad of his thumb rough against the sensitive flesh hidden by my folds. Beginning slowly, he circles my clit never touching it directly. Round and round he goes each pass winding my pleasure up another notch.

Those dark eyes never lose their focus. He is immune to my whimpers and my pleas. I come in a rush, liquid heat dripping from my core. No words of praise or filth greet my ears.

Andrew's pupils grow until the blue of his iris is barely visible. After my second orgasm he leans in and sucks my clit into his mouth without any warning. Barely a second of warm wet pressure on the bundle of nerves and I come with a scream clutching at the blankets beneath me. I try to speak but all I hear is incoherent babbling.

Three orgasms and I am done. I can't take anymore.

I pull and yank on Andrew's dark hair until his mouth releases my clit with an audible pop. Convinced he is done, I release his hair and relax back against the couch. The first lick jolts me upright.

A harsh grip on my hips keeps my butt pinned to the couch, splayed open for his enjoyment. He's vocal again. His sounds and words of praise are muffled by the sensitive pink folds of my pussy. A delicate humming sound sends vibrations through my core and my entire body tenses as I come again.

"Please," I beg. "No more. I can't take another."

"Do you remember your safe word?" Andrew asks as he pulls away.

His mouth and chin are shiny with the evidence of my arousal, but his eyes are laser focused on my face. Looking for signs of discomfort, I realize. During our chats on SoulConnect's app we each chose a safe word. A word we could use at any time to immediately stop any sexual activity.

Mine is carrots, the one vegetable I've never liked, and Andrew chose pineapples. Same category he said when I asked his reasoning.

"Yes," I reply slightly breathless.

Andrew arches a dark brow as he looks at me and waits. We stare at each other for a beat of time and then another. It soon becomes clear he's going to sit there as motionless as a statue until I either use my safe word or give verbal consent.

"I don't need to use my safe word," I tell him directly. "I want to continue."

He doesn't reply verbally, just leans down to give me a sweet kiss that tastes like a mixture of the mint candy he ate on the plane and my own musk. Distracted by his mouth and very wicked tongue I gasp in shock when he pushes his cock inside me. The grin on his face when he pulls away is dark and devious.

Not waiting for me to adjust he moves quickly as he begins to drive his cock into me in a brutal rhythm. I'm helpless to do more than take it. My hands scrabble for purchase on his shoulders, my nails digging in as I slide up the couch. Andrew pulls me back, impaling me on his cock and I reach over my head to push against the arm of the couch. Holding myself in place I watch as Andrew grabs my ankles and lifts them over one shoulder.

The new angle allows him to slide impossibly deeper, each pump of his hips working the breath from my body.

"Such a lovely little girlfriend, taking my cock like you were made for it," Andrew growls above me.

I can't answer between gasps, but he doesn't need a response.

"Made to be fucked by me," he says a second later.

I let out some shrill sound that he takes as agreement.

"Yes," he groans. "Listen to that."

He closes his eyes and tilts his head back as he continues to pound into me. A look of bliss softens his expression as he listens to the wet slap of our bodies colliding.

The obscene sounds combine with the harsh grip of his fingers biting into the flesh of my hip to drive me higher. Unable to stop it, I come crying Andrew's name as my muscles squeeze and milk his cock.

"That's it, Babe. Take every drop," he says hips pulsing as his seed coats my walls in warm spurts.

We lie in a boneless heap, the blankets beneath my back clinging to our sweaty skin as we catch our breath.

"Chinese," he says later.

It takes entirely too long for me to realize what he's talking about. Wordlessly I point at the fridge.

Sweet and sour chicken for me and cashew beef for him with a side of vegetable rolls to split. Andrew dutifully orders the food without complaint, amusement curling his lips when I make him answer the door. My refusal to put on clothes until the food arrives causes his eyes to darken with lust once more but he keeps his hands to himself until after dinner.

Over the next two weeks we fall into a comfortable routine. Each morning I wake up after Andrew to find him cooking breakfast before I leave for work, and he sets up his laptop in the living room.

After the first week I tidy up my incomplete projects and offer him the spare room as an office space for him to work in. After work I either cook dinner or we order takeout, and we watch TV together. Sometimes it's fantasy or sci-fi that we watch and other times it's trashy reality TV that my friends have me hooked on. And then we fuck like bunnies. No place in my tiny apartment is safe. We discover the kitchen table I got from Ikea that I always thought was flimsy is sturdy enough to bear my weight.

Andrew doesn't mention returning to Colorado and I'm too fucking scared to ask if he's staying. I want him to stay but every time I try to bring it up the words choke in my throat. And how crazy is that? It's barely been two weeks. It's too soon to ask a man to move in with me. Way too crazy.

But it feels like he's already moved in. He fixed my door the first day while I was at work. My key now turns easily in the lock, so I don't have to fight my door every day and the hinges no longer creak. Then he unclogged the shower drain without complaining about the excessive amount of hair he pulled out. Day by day he did little bits of maintenance to make my home more comfortable and not once did he call attention to it. And now I'm trying not to read too much into it. Trying not to assume it's an act of love.

Doesn't stop me from wanting to ask though. Doesn't stop me from wanting to tell him that I love him, and I never want him to leave. Doesn't stop the tension from melting out of my body each time I come home to find him wrapping up his work or folding a pile of laundry. His neat folds are precise in a manner my hands will never achieve.

It's insane. Completely.

"You did what?" Jill asks in a voice approaching shrill.

I look around and apologize to the tables near us with a sheepish expression. Even sitting outside on the patio of our favorite restaurant we can't be *that* loud. I joined my two friends for lunch. They were getting fussy that I cancelled on girl's night last week and I've missed them. And I haven't told them about Andrew yet. Hence Jill's tone.

"I met a man on a dating app-" I begin to reply, and she cuts me off with a dismissive wave.

"I heard you," Jill says her dark gaze pinning me in place before she swings her head to look at Gabriella. "Did you hear her? That she met a stranger online and didn't tell anyone that she was flying out to meet him?"

Gabriella tilts her head, her red ponytail following the movement as she looks at me appraisingly.

"I heard her," she tells Jill.

Jill's dark brown hair is pinned in a perfectly flawless bun, not a strand out of place.

"He could have been an axe murderer!" she whisper shouts mindful of the crowded patio.

"He's not," I argue. "He's sweet and he's a total weirdo but not in a bad way."

Jill stares at me, her eyes wide in disbelief. Gabriella sips her coffee as her gaze darts back and forth between us, gauging the level of tension.

"At least you came back safely," Jill mutters after a minute. "Can't believe you didn't let us vet him before you went out there to meet him."

Ignoring Jill's muttering Gabriella turns to me.

"It's been two weeks since you got back. Was the sex really that good that you're still hung up on this stranger you'll never see again?"

I clam up fast. Jill drops a chip back onto her plate as both women eye me with piercing looks.

"You'll never see him again, right?" Jill asks. "I mean he's in Colorado."

"Long distance?" Gabriella asks with a gleam in her eye.

Ever since she met Oliver, she's been more of romantic than ever before. You never know when you're going to meet your soulmate, she says all the time. Meeting her husband in a rideshare mix up right before Christmas, her favorite holiday, has her meddling in our love lives more than ever before.

"He's visiting," I say in a small voice.

"Visiting? Like for a weekend?" Gabriella asks. "Are you trying to do long distance then?"

It's Jill who sees the truth before I can say it. She's always been perceptive. Too perceptive.

"He came back with you," she says. "He's been here two weeks, and you haven't introduced us?"

"Is it true?" Gabriella squeals bouncing in her seat with excitement. "Can we meet him? Is he a ghoul head too?"

"Does he even have a job?" Jill cuts in over Gabriella's rambling.

"He works remotely," I tell them first to soften the protective rage simmering inside Jill.

"Does he pay rent?" Jill asks.

"We haven't talked about it-" I start to reply.

"That fucking bum!" she shouts and no longer caring about the people around us I find my temper rising.

"Stop it!" I shout back and she reels back in her seat no doubt shocked by my tone.

"He's not a bum. I haven't brought up bills because I haven't asked him how long he's staying. He buys groceries and orders takeout for both of us. He fixes all the little things around the apartment that I haven't been able to get maintenance to look at yet. The faucets. The drains. Hell, he even installed an additional lock on my door to make it safer," I rant until I feel blue in the face.

She's skeptical and I can understand why. It sounds outlandish and ridiculous from an outsider's perspective. But she hasn't met Andrew. She hasn't spent the last two weeks falling in love with the perfect man. Not that he would be perfect for Jill. She would murder him before her first Monday morning meeting. But for me, he is perfect.

"He likes Halloween," I add after a second.

Not as much as I do of course. My apartment is heavily decorated for the upcoming holiday, but his house didn't have a single pumpkin or fake cobweb to be found.

"We're meeting him," Jill says with a steely tone.

"He sounds like a keeper," Gabriella adds with a warm smile.

I don't mention that if I didn't want them to meet him, I wouldn't have brought him up. But he's quickly becoming an irreplaceable part of my life, and I want him to meet my friends. We make plans for the weekend, a nice dinner at my apartment so that I have time to prepare him for Jill's animosity and Gabriella's optimism.

There's no more dodging the subject now. We have to define our relationship before Jill launches an interrogation that would make the CIA nervous.

Andrew

"How long are you staying?" the petite brunette asks as she storms past me when I open the apartment door.

I could protest, but that would only drag this out. I know without asking that this fiery woman is Jill, and she is here to bust my balls. I'm about to close the door and answer her impertinent question when a second woman with red hair waltzes through the door.

"Nice to meet you, Andrew," Gabriella says as she brushes past me.

"Likewise," I mutter after glancing down the hallway to ensure that all my interrogators are present.

Emma's friends are easy to recognize from the photos littered around her apartment. Photos from conventions with Jill pinned to the fridge and a group photo with Jill,

Gabriella, and her husband Oliver from last Christmas framed on the mantel.

"So?" Jill asks spinning on her heel in the living room to face me with a fierce glare.

She has her hip cocked and an impatient frown on her face as she waits for my reply.

"As long as she'll let me," I answer.

"Oh my God!" Jill shouts. "You're sleeping with her so you can stay here!"

Her eyes are wide and she's pointing her finger at me like a tattling sister who has caught me red handed stealing cookies.

"No!" I shout back. "I have a home in Colorado!"

Her accusation is outlandish at best, but I don't need her undermining my relationship at the starting line. We stare at each other in silence for a few minutes before she turns away.

Just like that I watch her make herself at home in my girlfriend's apartment. Heels kicked under the coffee table she tucks her stocking covered feet underneath herself as she settles on the couch. She even fluffs my favorite pillow before settling against it. It's black with an orange cat silhouette that I find ridiculously charming.

"So, this is serious," Gabriella says from the kitchen where she has grabbed a pair of wine glasses.

She's not asking. She also isn't yelling like her friend, so I treat her statement like a question. One I take seriously.

"I want to marry her."

It's the first time I've said it out loud. Jill and Gabriella both turn to look at me with wide eyes, but I don't care that it's barely been a couple of weeks. The words coat my feverish skin like a cool balm. This is right and it feels good to say it outright. Emma and I are meant for each other. Today, a week from now, or two years will make no difference. I know she's the one for me.

"You just met," Jill counters, voicing the concern that has plagued my mind since Colorado.

"That's why I haven't proposed," I explain. "And I need to get a ring."

I know we belong together, but I also know that Emma needs time. I can give her time. I just can't give her fifteen hundred miles of distance.

"This is crazy," Jill mutters as she accepts a glass of red wine from Gabriella.

"Love is crazy," Gabriella tells her as she sits down on the couch beside her.

They're looking at each other and not at me. I watch as eyebrows raise, and frowns turn into smiles. It's like the pair of them are carrying on a silent conversation which I am not privy to.

It's not something that would normally bother me. But since they knocked on the door, I have been the topic of conversation. My reasoning and my intentions. My very presence. And now I'm being left out of the conversation. One which could affect my relationship with Emma.

"I'm not a psycho. Not a serial killer. I just want to be with Emma. Share our days with each other. I don't want to hear about what she had for lunch from fifteen hundred miles away. I want to hear it while we sit down for dinner. I love her."

"You love me?"

Emma

Andrew's shoulders tense under his faded blue shirt at my question. I can't see his face, but I can see over his shoulder the way Jill and Gabriella smirk at my interruption. Thanks to his work on the door, he didn't hear me come into the apartment until it was too late.

Turning his back on my friends, I'm startled by the look on his face. The determined set of his eyes looking at me with a vulnerable sort of hope combined with the way his mouth is set in a serious line. Neither smiling nor frowning. For the first time since we met, he looks nervous.

Out of his depth. Floundering with no grip on the outcome of this conversation, he looks worried.

I shouldn't be surprised to find my friends came over and cornered him without my knowledge. But I can't muster up the energy to be upset that they ignored my timeline, not when I came home to the best surprise. Even if I couldn't see the look on his face the first time he said those words. I heard them and felt their echo in my heart.

"I love you, Emma," he says. His blue eyes are dark with emotion. "I know it's crazy fast, I know you need time, but my heart doesn't beat without you near."

My words pile in my throat stealing the air from my lungs as my vision blurs. Every moment I've spent second guessing myself was in vain. Every step of the way this man was at my side. Not only physically but also emotionally.

As crazy as it may seem, we are on the same page. From that very first day we've been in sync.

"Andrew," I say between choked breaths. "It's not crazy. I love you too."

A single step is all it takes. I'm in Andrew's arms the fabric of his shirt soft against my cheek as his arms wrap around me and squeeze me tightly to his chest.

"Gag," Jill mutters to herself.

I hear the faint sound of Gabriella shushing her as Andrew rocks us back and forth. Without stepping away I wordlessly point at the door. Gabriella's giggles meld with Jill's quiet huffs of laughter as they leave. On the way out the door Jill slaps Andrew's back in farewell.

"Take care of our girl," Gabriella says just before they shut the door.

"I will," Andrew says to me. "Forever and ever I will."

Andrew

"Forgive me, Daddy for I've been naughty," Emma says as she presses her palms together and dips her head as if in prayer.

The beaded rosary wrapped around her right hand is a step further in this sacrilegious roleplay. I love the little details she's added to our costumes for this year's Halloween. It's been a week since we confessed our love for each other. I didn't think it could get any better but every day I swear I fall a little more in love with my Emma.

"Pray tell little one," I say. "What sins have you committed?"

I tip her chin up with my finger so that I can see her face. I'm seated on the bench seat at the end of our bed dressed as a priest, complete with cassock and cross.

"My dreams are filled with temptation," Emma says in a demure manner. "I dare not tell you the details or you shall think me wicked."

"I need to know the particulars so that I can decide your penance," I reply.

I stroke the side of her face gently with the back of two fingers as she smiles timidly at me. She is kneeling in front of me dressed in a nun's habit complete with a veil that hides her hair from me and frames her face in white.

Such a pretty little bride of Christ my girlfriend makes.

"I cannot tell you," she says letting her gaze drop to the ground at my feet. "But perhaps I could show you."

I let her words hang for a moment, pretending to consider her proposition. Leaning down until our faces are an inch apart, I confess my own secret.

"You tempt me like no other. Use me to confess your own sin and make me guilty of yet another. I lust. I covet."

Her hands slide up my thighs. Closer and closer they creep to where my cock is sitting hard as granite. I reach down to pull her up until she is seated in my lap.

"If we must sin, and sin we must, let it be worth the penance."

I capture her lips with mine as she melts so sweetly against me. Every curve of her body pressing into me as my cock grows impossibly harder aching to be buried deep inside her until her wet warmth wraps around the length.

"Like this?" she asks as her fingers unbutton the fly front cape of my cassock.

"It's a start. Remember you are meant to show me the wickedness that tempts you, not the crosses of lustful burden I bare," I murmur as she removes my white collar and exposes my bare chest to her wandering hands.

Without warning she stands and begins to remove her habit. The veil remains as the rest of her outfit falls to the hardwood floor.

"Naughty little nun," I mutter as I take in her naked curves.

"Perverted priest," she retorts with a quiet laugh as she strokes a hand over my cloth covered cock.

"Be a good girl, Sister Emma," I say in a warning tone. "Penance can quickly become punishment."

"Oh, no," she says bringing her palm up to cover her open mouth in a blatant display of false shock. "Whatever will I do?"

"Apparently you'll be taking sacrament on your knees," I say standing up and letting my cassock fall to the floor, exposing the jutting length of my cock as I do.

Silently she sinks down, kneeling on the puddle of our clothing to cushion her knees. Her lips pop open without fanfare and I let out a shaky breath as she takes me in her mouth.

Her lips stretch wide as she takes me slowly. The curve of her tongue stroking the underside of my cock as I sink deeper into her wet mouth.

"Naughty," I groan as I sink into the hilt. Her mouth is so warm and wet and when she sucks on my length my knees nearly buckle.

My hands reach out to grab her hair, but my fingers find the stiff fabric of her veil instead. The mischievous glint in her eye is all the proof I need that she left it on to thwart me. She bobs her head twirling her tongue around the mushroom shaped head as she pulls away.

I rake my fingers through my own hair as Emma works my cock. Every muscle in my body is tense as she carries out her own form of punishment. As I feel my release draw closer, I step back pulling my cock out of her mouth in the process.

"Surely there is more?" I ask as I try to focus.

"You'll be so disappointed with me," she replies.

"Never," I say in a harsher tone than our little scene calls for and she knows it.

Her eyebrow rises in reproach, but she doesn't address the odd tone. The topic is too heavy for the moment and better ignored for now. I don't want her to ever think that she isn't everything I need. I can never be disappointed with her even in jest.

"Have I tempted you?" she asks as she stands.

I watch her slim fingers play with the end of her veil in a similar manner to the way she plays with her hair when she wants to appear coy.

"Always," I say breaking character once again as I reach out to pull her body flush with mine.

Her skin is cool against mine. As she wraps her arms around my neck to pull me down for a kiss, I fall a little more in love with her. Ever since that first day we've just clicked. Not just sexually but in a truly meaningful way. Yes, the sex is off the charts but so is everything else.

We have no secrets, and no hidden shames. She accepts me just the way I am, and I accept her just the same. One day soon I'm going to get down on one knee and ask her to marry me. And I hope like hell she doesn't say it's too soon.

"Pray for our forgiveness," I order and wait for her to bring her palms together in front of her chest.

Bending down I grabbed the rosary that she dropped to the floor. Her eyes pop open as I begin wrapping the prayer beads around her wrists. The heat within her gaze is ratcheting up my own desire.

When I release her hand, she gives an experimental tug to test the knot. I watch as she moves each of her fingers before she gives the nod of approval. I grab her waist and toss her gently on the bed.

"Pray for our very souls," I whisper as I climb onto the bed between her thighs.

Emma eyes twinkle in the low light, the light green changing into the dark green of a placid lake. She murmurs a softly spoken prayer as I enter her swiftly, no mercy in my approach or my touch. Her hands strain against the rosary as she tries to touch me, but the bind holds. My rose covered hand pins hers above her head and with her blonde hair in a wild halo around her she looks every inch the virginal sacrifice.

Her moans sound like the sweetest prayer as I plunder her body. Nipples arching towards my mouth and thighs wrapping around my hips to pull me deeper she seeks control even as she lies helpless beneath me.

"Divine," I praise as her moans get higher in pitch and her walls begin to flutter around my length.

"Open wide, Sister Emma," I growl. "And receive my blessing."

On cue she clamps down on my cock, her muscles milking me as she comes around my cock. Eyes rolling back as she arches her back, every muscle in her body tenses as she cries out.

Thrusting steadily, I don't let up, watching her fall apart under me, as I continue to hammer my hips into hers. Gritting my teeth I try in vain to hold back, but when she hooks her ankles behind my back and peers up at me from under her eyelashes I spiral out of control.

"Give it to me," she pleads, her full lips parted and her eyes soft. "Come for me, Babe."

Helpless to resist I come with her name whispered on my lips as she takes every drop of my seed with a lusty smile on her face.

"Best Halloween, ever," she says later while we lie cuddled together.

"Yet," I correct with a gentle pat to her ass. "I'm already planning for next year."

Her soft laughter lulls me to a languid state before I drift off to sleep, the gentle press of her lips to my jaw the last thing I remember before darkness takes me.

Epilogue

Emma

Six Months Later

Forty minutes into our hike, Andrew tugs me to an overlook. The trail we're on is coated in pine needles and tall grass grows between towering trees on both sides. It's not the most picturesque trail we've explored in Georgia but the view at the top of the mountain is supposed to be stunning.

Sweaty with my tank top sticking to my back, I'm happy for a respite. It may be April but it's already gearing up to be a scorching summer. Today more than any other I'm glad I moved to Colorado with Andrew. It might have its downsides, but I prefer the snow to the blazing heat and the solitude of our cabin compared to my old apartment.

We're back visiting family and friends. Andrew made a smashing impression on my family all those months ago. My own brother claims Andrew will get him in the breakup. The jerk.

Panting to catch my breath, I step onto the grass covered cliff looking down at the mountain range around us and the sea of trees covering them so that they look like green waves.

"It's pretty," I say to Andrew.

He picked this trail, and I don't want him to think I'm disappointed with his selection. There's no one around for miles and we only have the chirping birds and squirrels for company out here. Other trails may have better vistas, but I like the break in our trip.

We've been surrounded by people all week. Dinners and game nights as we try to pack in as much time with everyone as possible before we leave for home. When Andrew doesn't respond right away, I turn to look at him and find him kneeling behind me with an open ring box clutched between fingers turning white at the tips.

"Emma," he begins before pausing, every emotion visible in his eyes as he takes a deep breath and audibly swallows.

"Will you marry me?" he asks.

For a moment we're frozen in time. I can feel every beat of my heart blasting like a bass drum. It's like forgetting how to breathe as tears fill my eyes and I nod rapidly choking on my answer.

"Yes," I manage to say between breaths.

Our bodies collide a moment later, my arms wrapping around his neck and pulling him down for a kiss that starts sweet and ends utterly filthy.

"It will be a lengthy engagement," I tell him after we break apart.

His lips are red from my nibbles, and I love the slightly drunk look that he always gets after we kiss.

"In case you change your mind?" he asks with a cheeky grin.

"No!" I say slapping his chest. "To plan the perfect wedding."

"And honeymoon," Andrew adds and I can't resist rolling my eyes.

"Of course," I nod before I see a mischievous glint sparkle in his eye.

This late in the afternoon and this trail is empty of people. I'm sure that's why Andrew picked this one instead of another in this national park.

"Run," he growls. "I'm going to chase you and when I catch you, I'm going to breed your sweet little pussy raw."

I spin on my heel and begin running back down the mountain. The path is packed dirt that slides underneath my tennis shoes, but I make good progress. Faster than running up the trail, I'd be out of breath before I reached the next overlook. I hear Andrew's heavy footsteps behind me are louder than the heartbeat pounding in my ears. Stronger and faster, he closes in fast before letting me slip away at the last second.

I'm panting with exertion but he's not even slightly winded as he darts in close again. The way he toys with me only excites me as he makes a playful grab for my arm. Then as we pass a bend in the trail, he makes his move.

One moment I'm running down the trail and the next he has whisked me off my feet. Ignoring my fists beating onto his back he carries me into a clearing.

"Too slow," Andrew growls into my ear as he sets me down. "Did you really think you could escape me?"

I try to stand but a quick yank on my ankle has me sprawled out beneath him again. Wordlessly he uses his hold on my leg to flip me over onto my stomach.

"I'll do anything-" I begin to plead when Andrew shoves my head down to the forest floor.

Wet leaves stick to my face as I hear the clink of Andrew's belt buckle as it hits the ground.

"You'll do nothing," he says. "You'll lie down and take my cock like the pretty little prey you are."

"Or what?" I ask as his hands wrench my leggings down to my knees where he leaves them.

"Or nothing," he growls. "You're mine to fuck as I please."

I can't help the moan that slips out of my mouth as he squeezes my ass in a punishing grip.

"I'm going to fuck this cunt until it is swollen and dripping with my seed."

His fingers stroke over my damp panties as I bite my lips to keep quiet.

"Dirty little girl," he purrs as he teases my outer lips through the underwear. "You're wet just from thinking about my cock plowing into your juicy little pussy."

The strike comes out of nowhere. His hand slapping my pussy with enough force to sting, causing me to yelp.

"Naughty," he says.

My damp panties briefly cling to my skin as he peels them down to join my leggings.

"Look at this pretty little cunt, already dripping for my cock." He runs a rough finger lightly through my folds just teasing my entrance without entering.

His hand wraps in my hair using his grip on the strands to pull my head up. My scalp stinging from the rough yank, my vision goes blurry with tears.

"Beg for it," he snarls with his chin resting on my shoulder.

Seated like we are the head of his cock is nudging my entrance. I wiggle backwards trying to tempt him into plunging his length inside me.

"*Beg*," he orders giving my hair a sharp tug in reproach, his voice a deep rumble that sends a fluttering pulse deep inside my core.

I want to deny him. See how far I can push him until he breaks. The sharp sting of his hand striking my ass has me reconsidering.

"Please," I say in my sweetest voice.

The hand in my hair twists tighter until the tingling of my scalp is bordering on true pain.

"Please. What," he bites out his breath hot on my ear.

"Please fuck me," I cry. "Fuck me like the dirty whore I am."

"Good girl," he croons before he nudges the head of his cock into my entrance.

I almost scream with frustration when he stops. The hand wrapped around his cock that's sandwiched between his thigh and my ass pulls away.

"Andrew," I plead as his hands grip my hips, the pads of his fingers biting into my flesh with a brutal grip.

He doesn't respond. Without warning he uses his hold on me to slam my hips down. His cock plunges into me fully to the hilt in one stroke. His grip controls my body raising and slamming me back down on his cock while I try to help. The wet squelch of our bodies meeting only grows louder as he works me on his length.

I come apart screaming his name, startling a nearby flock of birds that leap into flight cawing their reproach.

He pauses long enough to reach around and grab my throat with a firm hand.

"Feeling good Emma?" he asks in a mocking tone. "Was that good for you?"

I nod enthusiastically trying to steady my breathing between gasps.

"How lovely," he purrs squeezing my throat for a moment as he licks my cheek. "I'm so happy that was good for *you*."

His hand releases my throat, and I draw in a shaky breath. The muscles in my legs tremble as he runs a rough hand along the inside of my thigh. His fingers find my clit, his touch slick from my arousal as he pinches the sensitive nub between his thumb and finger.

"Ah," I gasp my back arching as he pinches it twice, the second press of his fingers lingering longer.

The pain fades leaving a warm feeling of awareness behind as Andrew reaches between us to press a strong palm to my back. I bend over, my hot face returning to the leaf covered ground.

Andrew shifts to his knees, even the small adjustment causing his cock to move inside me drawing a soft moan from my lips.

"I'll never get tired of seeing how this wet little pussy looks wrapped around my cock," he says as he pulls away before thrusting back into me.

"Mine. Say it," he growls as he pulls away, almost his entire length leaving me as he plants a foot beside my knees.

The next thrust goes impossibly deeper as his grip on my hips turns bruising.

"*Mine*," he snarls, his word a claiming and an order.

"Yours," I cry as he hammers his cock into me.

He pays no attention to my cries as he drives his hips into mine over and over. I come on his cock screaming his name with my muscles clenching and trying flutily to lock him in place.

Paying me no heed his pace remains consistent, not allowing me to come down from one orgasm before he sends me spiraling into another.

"Emma. Fuck," he groans as his hips stutter to a halt, his fingers squeezing my sides as he comes coating my walls with sticky warm seed.

He pulls back his limp cock dangling as we both right our clothes. With dirt on my hands and knees I know I look a fright, but nothing can wipe the satisfied grin from my face.

"Love you my pretty little wife to be," Andrew says just before he kisses me.

Epilogue II

Emma

Three Years Later

"Beautiful day for a wedding," Andrew says as we take our seats next to Gabriella and Oliver. Gabriella is six months pregnant with a swollen belly that enters the room before she does, and Oliver is beside himself with worry anytime she's on her feet for more than five minutes.

"Still can't believe Jill didn't want any kind of wedding party," Oliver mutters to himself as much as us.

"She's always been independent," Gabriella says before adding as she gestures to her stomach. "I'm just glad I don't have to fit all of this into chaffron and tulle."

"Does he mean to look so arrogant?" Andrew murmurs to me eyes fixed ahead on the man standing beside the priest.

I can't argue that Alan does look a tad arrogant. I'm not sure if it's the smirk or his posture that screams superiority, but I suspect it's both.

"Yes," I reply. "He and Jill are a perfect match."

"I was happy to see her taken down a few pegs," he confides in a whisper that makes Oliver chuckle.

"Karma," he agrees.

"Shush. The pair of you I swear! They are a wonderful couple," I chide in a whisper mindful of the people seated around us.

"You made me wait an eternity," Andrew complains. "They've been engaged a month."

"Less than two years after you proposed we got married," I reply. "And our wedding was worth the wait."

Andrew's soft smile is the only agreement I need. He remembers our wedding day as fondly as I do. The pre-ceremony fuck in the dressing room. The lace dress that he peeled off my body later that night. And then the honeymoon that Andrew planned for us in the Caribbean.

"I would have worn the blue tux if you had agreed to an elopement," Andrew says right before the wedding march begins playing.

I turn to give him a frosty glare to find him grinning from ear to ear. I know he's trying to fire me up. I know all his tricks at this point but damn me if they don't still work.

The devilish bastard was perfectly agreeable on everything except for two things. The cake flavor and his attire. I tried for months to convince him to wear a navy blue tux that I thought he would look delicious in. In the end the cake was red velvet with cream cheese frosting, and he wore a black suit with a blue tie.

I'll die before I admit that the tux wouldn't have looked as good as the suit. He knows that I know it. But I won't give him the satisfaction of telling him so. His tattooed hand grabs mine, the floral bouquet on my skin blending beautifully with his roses as we stand to watch Jill walk down the aisle on the arm of Alan's dad.

For now, we'll be proper but later I'm going to tie him to the bed and fuck that attitude out of him. He'll shut up and take that strap on like a good boy if I have anything to say about it.

The End

Eager to find out what happens to Tobias Carmichael, the towering lumberjack son of a baker? Check out Sugar Mapleor meet all three Carmichael brothers in Lumberjacks in Love: The Complete Series.

Printed in Dunstable, United Kingdom